SNOWED IN FLING

A Steamy New Year's Novella

G. MARIE

Snowed in Fling

Copyright © G. Marie 2022

All rights reserved.

First published in 2022

No part of this book may be reproduced, stored in a retrieval system or transmitted in any form or by any means, without the prior permission in writing of the publisher, nor be otherwise circulated in any form of binding or cover other than that in which it is published and without a similar condition, including this condition, being imposed on the subsequent purchaser. All characters in this publication other than those clearly in the public domain are fictitious, and any resemblance to real persons, living or dead, is purely coincidental.

Cover Design By: Cover Apothecary at www.coverapothecary.com

Editor: Brittni Van at Overbooked Author Services

This book is dedicated to my mom. She instilled in me a love of books and holidays, and encouraged me to chase my dreams.

Content Warning

This book contains brief mentions of past parental loss.

1

Jade

New Year's Eve, Eve

INSTEAD OF KICKING off my week-long staycation by gently waking up cozy in my bed, surrounded by pillows and drowning under a soft comforter, watching all the saved holiday baking shows on my DVR, I'm struggling to get my ass ready for work. That's right, work.

"Folks, this blizzard is going to come in hard and fast today. Forecasts are showing the Aspen area will get hit starting around 3pm."

I can't help but giggle at the meteorologist on the TV - *hard and fast*. It's the only bright spot to my morning as I dig through my wardrobe to find something presentable to wear. All that's left is the one cocktail dress I own, a few t-shirts and leggings. It's been laundry day for at least a week.

After three months of hardly a day off, I'm supposed to be on vacation for the next week. A whole week at home to catch up on sleep, chores and reading. It's my idea of heaven. But instead, my client, Eli Fox, called me at 6:00am demanding that with the sale of his company and the formation of the foundation he's starting all converging right after the new year, he needed me to come in and work. And by come in, it means trekking my butt way up the mountain to his luxury ski chalet. Boasting over 7,000 square ft., he's turned one wing into an office space for the both of us.

I was also hoping to use this time away from Eli's stupidly handsome face, that sits atop his even more stupidly sexy body, to fall out of love with him.

But alas, that wasn't to be. I knew from the day I walked into his home, tripped over my two left feet, only to have him catch me — holding on for a moment too long before letting me go - that I was in too deep. The way his emerald green eyes widened and burned into me. The sharp cut of his jawline, highlighted by his closely cut beard, and the way his lips pressed together, almost in a grimace. He looked annoyed and surprised all at once.

And that's how I, Jade Williamson, fell in love at first sight. Just like in the movies and books. It's pretty silly if you ask me.

First of all, he's so far out of my league it's not even funny. I've seen the headlines all asking *When will Silicon Valley's Most Eligible Bachelor Settle Down?*

Second, the staffing company I work for, the Aspen Concierge Service, expressly forbids romantic relationships with clients. It's in the contract I signed as Eli Fox's executive assistant.

Need housekeeping? Personal chef? Personal Trainer? Done. Or in my case, a person who makes your life go round? The ACS has you covered. I do everything from reviewing and editing contracts to making coffee. And I do it pretty damn well. So well, in fact, my boss told me during my last review I could be up for a promotion.

While I'm not quite living paycheck to paycheck, that'll all change when my best friend and roommate, Katie, moves to California with her fiancé in a few months. I've been desperately trying to find a new roommate, but no luck so far. Most of those who work seasonally at the resorts will have left by then. Those that are left, the year-rounders like me, already seem to be set with housing.

Hence the reason I'm working my ass off, spending day in and day out with a man whose presence sets my nerves on edge, all to get a freaking promotion. Which I deserve, by the way.

I finally settle on my favorite pair of leggings paired with a slouchy hunter green sweater and rush into our small kitchen and try to enjoy a quiet cup of coffee.

I scoop the last of our Christmas spice grinds into the coffee maker and hit brew just as Katie emerges from her room.

"Urrgh," she mumbles, rubbing her eyes as she stumbles towards the kitchen.

I can't help but laugh when I see her oversized t-shirt depicting a ripped and disturbingly hot Santa leering at me. The only words are in bright gold font saying, *Sit on My Face*.

"Morning, Sunshine."

"Coffee, first. Please."

The ding of the coffee machine alerts me that it's done. The magical smell of warm cinnamon, maple and chocolate permeates the entirety of our tiny apartment.

I fill both our mugs to the brim, before grabbing the tin of leftover cookies I made Christmas Eve. Peanut butter and chocolate kiss cookies as well as sugar cookies. I've been on a steady cookie diet for the last week, and I have zero regrets.

"Those couldn't possibly be good anymore," Katie says as she takes a sip and plops down on the couch. She's right — they're stale, crumbling the minute I dunk them into my steaming mug. Doesn't stop me from moaning the minute I bite into one and the explosion of butter and sugar instantly makes me happy. The holidays are my favorite time of year. They remind me of growing up with a mom who always made a big deal about them, especially Christmas. These are both her recipes, and I can't bring myself to throw away the leftovers.

"What are you doing up? I thought you were off for the next week." Katie pins me with a suspicious stare — taking in the fact I'm in something other than pajamas. She knows that on my rare days off, I sleep like the dead until 10am at least. She will give me shit as soon as she knows I agreed to go into work. So, I pretend like I don't hear her.

The live tree we purchased this year sits in front of the large picture window in our living room. With a view of the snow covered everything and mountains in the background, it's the perfect place for it. Despite our best efforts to keep it fresh, the branches have begun to droop and turn brown. No amount of fresh water could keep it from happening. Having the tree up while I spend New Year's Eve home alone tomorrow night, with my box of Mac-n-Cheese and $8 wine, seems extra sad.

The sound of Katie clearing her throat pulls me out of my musings. "Ebenezer called you into work, didn't he?"

"Look — I really want this promotion. When my contract with Eli is up…" I let my sentence trail off with a shrug. I know she's tired of me sounding like a broken record.

It doesn't help that Simon, owner of ACS and the signer of my paychecks, has told me repeatedly to keep Eli happy. And that if I succeed, the promotion is mine.

"Yea, yea. If I wasn't engaged, that man could get it. Anytime, any day of the week. I can just imagine him now. In a Santa hat and nothing else…," she says with a wink and a smirk, causing me to choke on my coffee. I haven't told her about my…crush. It's just too cliche, and I know she'll tease me endlessly while encouraging me to put myself out there and make a move.

"But seriously, I hate that we haven't found you a new roommate for when I leave. Are you sure you don't want me to stay a few extra months, just until you find someone? Plus, you don't even like working for the ACS. You're a writer, Jade. Be a writer."

"No, you've gotta go live your life. I can't just *be a writer* and nothing else. I need money to live." And to pay off the student loans I'm currently drowning in.

Another thing I was looking forward to during my vacation. Writing. I've wanted to be an author since I was a little girl. Fairy tales and fantasy were my escape when my mom passed away in middle school. Now as an adult, writing fantasy romance is my real passion. But to write full-time and self-publish? That takes money. Hence, the need for this promotion. I'll be able to cover my rent on my own, pay off my debt and save towards my dream.

Katie bounds up from the couch, her mug forgotten on the worn wooden coffee table to throw her arms around me in a tight hug. At least she'll be leaving the eclectic mix of second-hand furniture and art we've collected the last few years here, that way I won't need to replace anything. Our big gray couch has seen many movie and pizza nights, drunken cry fests and more than a few spills. Filled with cushy white pillows and fuzzy throw blankets, it's one of my favorite spots in our apartment.

"I just hate that he says jump and you say how high," Katie pouts.

"Eli or Simon?"

"Simon, of course. He's a massive asshole. He's just dangling this promotion like a carrot, thus making you kill yourself to please Mr. high maintenance up the mountain." I've heard this several times and know she'll burn out soon.

I pull her into a hug, "Careful, you'll hurt yourself falling off that soapbox."

Katie laughs while squeezing me back. "I'll miss you, bestie," she says as she backs away.

"Me too. But when you get back, it's you, me and sappy rom-coms right?"

Katie nods at me while I slip into my wool coat and tug on the brand-new leather gloves she got me for Christmas.

Just as I step outside the door, I hear her call out to me as she grasps the handle in her palm, "Maybe you should finally tell Eli how you feel, Jade. What do you really have to lose?"

I shouldn't be surprised she's figured out my secret. "Oh, I dunno. MY JOB? — a possible promotion? Pride? Self-worth? The list goes on."

Katie rolls her eyes, "Careful driving please. Your car is not built for Aspen weather. Also - don't do anything I wouldn't do." Her giggle and words are lost as she quietly shuts the door behind me before I can jokingly ask her what exactly she *wouldn't* do.

2

Jade

The drive to Eli's house was mostly uneventful. My tires lost traction once or twice on the fresh powder, but nothing I couldn't easily correct. I mentally add new snow tires to the endless list of expenses. Somewhere after college loans and credit card payments. Ugh.

I had to drive so slowly that now I'm 20 minutes late. I've heard a few text alerts and a phone call. It can only mean that Eli is wondering where I am.

I zip up my coat and race up the steps to the house trying to get out of the cold. Eli insisted on me having a key saying he couldn't be bothered to answer the door each day when I arrived. My frozen fingers fumble trying to insert the key when the door is jerked open. All 6'3" of Eli Fox stands before me, from the top of his expertly tousled inky black hair to the tips of his designer Italian leather dress shoes, perfect as always.

His brows are drawn together, and his jaw is clenched as he quickly peruses me, as though searching for an injury. Seeming satisfied that I'm fine, his fierce expression relaxes with relief, a small smile even pulls at his lips.

"Glad you could join me, Jade," he says with a smirk

before turning and walking towards the giant office space we share.

"Sorry I'm so late. It won't happen again," I say hurriedly, as I follow him and settle down at my workspace.

Was…was he worried about me? Obviously as a boss worries about an employee, Jade. Duh.

"Where are we with those six new contracts," Eli's deep voice breaks through my daydreaming.

Sigh. It's going to be a long day.

SIX HOURS later and I'm finally breaking for a late lunch. If I hustle through the last two contracts I'm reviewing for Eli, I can be out of here in the next two hours and then finally kick-off my vacation.

Just as I pull out all the things I need for a sandwich, I spot Eli walking through the living room, shirtless. Showing off smooth tan skin, stretched over a broad chest and perfectly sculpted muscles. Ones that rope his arms - the kind you know could hold you up against a wall as he thrusts himself…Umm, what?

Anyways, he has muscles - he's in shape. *PFFFT*, no big deal.

It's not just the physical attraction, though. He listens to me, my ideas. He encourages me to implement them and trusts me to do way more advanced work with the foundation setup than I ever thought I'd be doing. Learning about his vision for the foundation, witnessing how hard he works, and knowing he's not content to just swim in his money and do nothing else, are all reasons why I fell head over heels for him.

But anyways, who walks around half naked in December, in Aspen while outside? I've lived here for 10 years, and I'm still not quite used to the bone deep chill. My nipples could cut glass six months out of the year at least.

And OK - fine, maybe he's dressed that way because every afternoon at 4:00pm, after he works out in his state-of-the-art home gym, he finishes it off with swimming laps in the heated pool that sits outside, just off the kitchen and living room. The house is mostly open concept, and so the back wall is just windows creating that indoor-outdoor living feel. And right now, it's giving me a view I wish I could hate.

Instead, the only light outside is from the crackling fire pit and the formation of an early sunset which is casting just enough light to highlight all the shadows of his body as his arms move up and down out of the water, cutting across the placid water. He's been at it for 20 minutes and hasn't slowed down a bit.

I try to refocus on what I'm doing rather than panting after my boss. Cutting my hand and bleeding all over the place isn't something I want to experience. Pretty sure he already thinks I'm clumsy enough since I tripped the first time I met him.

One of the great things about working for Eli is that he keeps a fully stocked fridge and pantry. I never have to worry about meals when I'm here since one of the perks of the job is that I can help myself to whatever I want, whenever I want it. Too bad he's not on the menu.

The trill of my ringtone, a popular Christmas carol, breaks the silence in the kitchen as I see Katie's name and face flash on the screen. Eli is outside, so I feel safe to answer it on speaker.

"You're about to cut the tip of your finger off, aren't you?"

I peer down at the cutting board under my hands- a half-chopped carrot in various sizes because I was indeed not paying attention. I'd be annoyed if she wasn't right. "Good to know my reputation as a klutz is so well known. I think I can handle the basics of chopping. I learned from the best." The best being her, of course.

"So, you're not watching Eli right now during his mandatory swim break?"

Sometimes I wish I didn't tell my best friend everything. Then she wouldn't know about my feelings for Eli. Or that I sneak peeks of him while he's swimming.

I blow the hair that's worked its way out of my bun and into my eyes out of my face and resume chopping with the super sharp chef's knife. "Why are you calling again?"

"Can't a girl call her bestie?"

"You're making it sound creepy! Besides, I am not. It's not my fault he's a creature of habit and insists —" The sharp pinch of the knife coming down on the tip of my thumb proves that I'm clearly a liar, "Shit!" The clatter of the hand-forged titanium steel reverberates off the black quartz countertops.

I quickly suck on my finger - the metallic taste of blood filling my mouth. "Fuck, fuck, fuckity fuck."

"Ugh! Jade, I told you to always tuck your fingers! There's gotta be a first aid kit somewhere there." I'd forgotten that Katie was on the phone, but she clearly knows just from the sounds what I've done.

"Ughmmpf," I say around my finger that I'm currently still nursing to stem the flow of blood. "I gotta go! Have a safe flight, love ya," I shout before I hang up, not waiting for her response.

I turn the faucet to as cold as it can go in and quickly stick my whole hand under the rush of chilly water. If nothing else, it might numb the pain. I glance at the pool but it's empty now. I can only hope that Eli came inside and went straight to his room, so he doesn't witness this debacle. How embarrassing. I can hear the conversation now.

How'd you cut yourself, Jade?

I wasn't paying attention because I was too busy wishing you'd press your naked body up against mine.

Yes, perfect. Great conversation. Then I'd die of mortification.

Somewhere from deep in the house I hear a door open, and I know that means Eli is probably on his way in here. I scramble to wrap a few paper towels around my hand and rummage through the drawers trying to find the first aid kit. Surely even an uber wealthy guy like Eli Fox has a junk drawer?

"Shit, shit. Where the fuck is it?"

Before I get much farther, the deep, melodic and rich voice of none other than Eli Fox sends shivers down my spine.

"I must say, I didn't know you had such a dirty mouth, Jade," he says, casually leaning against the doorframe of the kitchen. Hands shoved into the pockets of plush gray sweatpants. *Because of course.* I can't stop my eyes from focusing on how the tight black t-shirt stretches across his chest - only serving to highlight the dips and swells of sleek muscles.

I slam the drawer I was currently raiding shut and yank my thumb out of my mouth, wrapping the towel back around it so I don't drip blood in front of my boss. Too late though - the towel itself is soaked in blood and when Eli sees it, his entire demeanor changes. Do I tell him that it's because I was too busy checking him out?

Before I can even get a word out, Eli is in front of me. The cocky grin wiped off his face. His brows furrowed as he narrows his eyes onto my injured hand. "What happened?" He murmurs gruffly at me while he gently pulls the towel I'm clutching away and draws my hand towards his chest. His head is bent down as he examines the wound, close enough that if I tilted my head up and back, stood on my tip toes, I'd be within reach of his mouth. At that very moment his eyes meet mine, and lord only knows what he sees staring back at him. But the corner of his mouth kicks up in a tiny smile. How much I want him to sit me on the counter, wrap my legs around his waist and unwrap me like a late Christmas gift.

He carefully guides my arm up into the air. "Elevate your hand a bit."

"Yes, sir," I reply. But instead of the mocking bite I was going for, I sound breathless. I blush. Hard. And look away, darting my eyes around hoping to lock on something, anything other than his face.

He grips my chin, directing my face back to him, his green eyes barreling into me, sweeping my face like he's never seen me before, "Hmm, good girl," he whispers. Like we're wrapped in a bubble together, despite no one else being here, it feels safer, more secure with his body so close to mine. His words dance through my mind and the tenor of his voice vibrates through my body.

"The housekeeper moved the first aid supplies to the laundry room. I'll be right back."

He rubs his thumb across the palm of my hand just as he takes a step closer to me. Both of his large, strong hands grip me at the waist, lifting me and sitting me back down onto the barstool to my right.

Offering me a stern glance, he instructs me with, "Don't move," before he disappears into the laundry room off the kitchen to grab the first aid kit.

Those two words slide down like hot honey, pooling as an ache builds in my core - making me pretty fucking happy that I'm sitting down. *Am I turned on by this?* I can't, because he's my boss. The guy my bosses answer to - being attracted to him is bad enough. But him *knowing* it? Defcon five.

I could just get up like an adult and go help him find the supplies. But those two words, *don't move*, have my ass glued to this barstool.

"There's enough supplies for an apocalypse in there, or a snowstorm at least." Eli says, walking back into the kitchen with a giant first aid kit, setting it down and methodically pulling out a band-aid, alcohol wipes and an antibiotic cream

- laying them all down in a row, in order of how he seems to be planning to use them.

"Your assistant must be pretty meticulous."

He grins but doesn't say anything as he pulls my hand onto the counter, laying it flat, but holding it firmly. I can't help but admire his hands. His assured grip. The palms of his hands are rougher than I thought they'd be, for someone who spends his life behind a computer.

I can't help but hiss and try to jerk my hand away as he cleans the wound with the alcohol wipes. "Stay still," he says as he leans down and blows on it, soothing the sting.

He keeps his head bent as he places the band-aid on. "You did so well." The deep rumble of his voice combined with the words of praise light me up in a way I didn't know I loved. Or needed.

My face is on fire. But not because I'm embarrassed but because I'm so turned on and worried he can sense it. He's got to know, right? Is he - is he flirting with me?

It must be the reason my brain short circuits and I lean up close enough to brush my lips against. *Holy shit, I just kissed my boss. What the hell, Jade!*

I freeze, waiting for him to react. Peering up at his eyes, I find that he's staring at me intensely, like there's a war going on inside his head. I start backing away slowly, realizing I've made a HUGE fucking mistake. Only as I move back, his hand comes up to cup my neck and he quickly pulls me back to him, capturing my lips, gently at first — brushing against them once, twice and finally he nips at my lower lip seeking entry.

Then the kiss becomes a claiming kind, like he wants to devour me. A tangle of tongues and clash of teeth as we both try to get closer. Every neuron in my body lights up like a freaking Christmas tree.

I've always wondered what it would be like to kiss Eli. Not even in my wildest dreams did I think it'd be this intense, this all-consuming. Running my hands along his waist, I push his t-shirt up so I can trail my hands up his back. I take a moment to revel in all the rolling and flexing muscles under smooth skin.

Eli breaks away first, the only sound our labored breaths as we both release each other. I'm scared to move, to ruin this moment. What's he thinking? Does he want to keep going? Does he regret it? I'm scared of what I'll see when I look at him.

I finally gather the courage to make eye contact and he's quickly moving away to the other side of the kitchen, packing away the kit. What? I can't even gather a coherent thought, and he's the only sign that we just mauled with his pinkened lips and flushed cheeks.

Not even looking up from his task he says coldly, "The snow is coming down pretty hard. That storm they've been calling for is starting. You probably want to get going before it gets worse."

Wherever the warm and flirty Eli from earlier came from, he's gone now. Replaced by the cool, collected man I've come to know. And love, like a big ol' dummy.

Every warm and fuzzy feeling I had chills at his words. I'm suddenly aware of how ridiculous I must look. Must seem to him. The arousal pulsing through me dies — mortification sets in as I realize what an idiot I am. I put the moves on my FREAKING BOSS, and yea he was into it for 2.5 seconds, but maybe that was just biology? Oh my god, I've gotta get out of here. I place my hand over my racing heart which is cracking as I quickly gather my coat and purse.

"Well - uh. Thank you for this." I wave my hand around lamely, showing off my bandaged finger.

Still not looking at me he just murmurs, "Mmhmm."

I button my coat all the way to my chin, armored and ready to face him. "I'm heading out. You should be fine for tomorrow. All the food for the weekend is prepped, the house is stocked. Happy New Year's Eli - I'll see you in a week."

He's just staring at me. No grin or smirk. Just a crease in his brows, as though he's trying to figure something out. I rock back on my heels, about to jump out of my skin, and I make a dash for the door.

"Jade?" I turn around, desperately hoping he asks me not to leave.

"Drive safe. And Happy New Year."

3

Jade

THE ONLY RADIO STATIONS I CAN TUNE INTO, ALL THE WAY UP this mountain, are the two that are playing Christmas music. The snow is falling fast and heavy and my windshield wipers aren't keeping up. I've been slowly weaving around the narrow and windy mountain road that leads back to my safe and warm condo downtown. A mile has taken 15 minutes since I'm moving at a snail's pace — riding my squeaky brakes the whole time. Which, yes, I know you're not supposed to do that. But knowing something and putting it into practice are two different things.

Three more miles to go.

I make this drive Every. Single. Day. It's one that my car can normally handle. But my snow tires are old - hell my car is old as dirt. And the sleet that has started to fall on top of the snow-covered ground and has frozen over into a goddamn glassy lake, where I'm now slipping and sliding while crawling at five miles an hour.

It doesn't help that the heat finally went out two weeks ago. Yet another thing I haven't had the time or money to fix in this car. Full of regrets at the moment — about so many things it seems.

"What a spectacularly shitty day, Jade. First you throw yourself at your boss, who gives you the best kiss of your life, before acting like nothing happened and rejecting you. And now you're going to freeze to death on this dark mountain road." I can't help but mutter to myself as my rear tires suddenly make the worst squealing noise I've ever heard. I can feel myself losing traction, drifting to the right.

Stay calm. Hold the wheel steady and gently direct it straight. And don't, no matter what you do, hit the brakes.

This is all well and good when you're not about to have a panic attack as you drift over to the side of the road that drops fuck only knows how many feet.

I can see the edge coming up. Nothing but trees weighed down by snow and ice and sheer drop into nothingness. This is not how I thought I'd die.

Fuck it. Self-preservation takes over and I jerk the wheel sharply to the left. Too sharply of course, which sends the tail of my car out spinning me 360 degrees.

Tires screeching, metal scrapes and glass shatters. I hear screaming, only to realize it's me. It all happens so fast that I can't stop myself from closing my eyes until - "OOMPF." Everything stops. Including me when the wheel stops my forward motion, crushing my boobs. "Goddamnit," I hiss in pain. The car rocks a little side to side from the impact of whatever I've landed in, or on.

"You're ok. You're ok. I'm ok," I say through panicked breaths. My heart threatens to jump out of my chest, and I'm scared to open my eyes. I peep one open and realize I'm facing the road backwards, looking at the incline that I just slid down. I'm on the left side of the road, the side of the car lined up against the giant spruce trees that stopped me. The passenger side of my car is crushed in just a little, but thank god none of it reached me.

I wiggle my toes and bounce my knees. Looking down I don't see any blood or anything that's hit me. My body aches a bit, probably from tensing up during the accident. But by some fucking miracle I'm ok. Except for the fact that my car is very much not ok, and I could've died.

But ya know, silver linings and all that.

I'm just over a mile from Eli's house, and I could walk but I didn't really wear the boots to walk in, especially at an incline like this and definitely not in these conditions. I pull out my phone, thinking of who to call. Katie is out of town. In fact, everyone in our little friend group is traveling. Fifteen minutes later I've hung up with my insurance company who tried to get me a tow. But the wait time is five hours at least because clearly, I'm not the only person in this mess right now.

As much as I don't want to, I call Simon. Even though he expressly told me that he's taking the holiday to spend time with his wife, who he's cheating on with two different women, and that I'm not to bother him. But the accident happened on company time, and I feel like I should alert him. And maybe he can come pick me up. As much as he's the last resort. Well, almost. As soon as the call goes straight to voicemail, I realize Simon rejected my call.

My only option is Eli fucking Fox.

4

Eli

SILICON VALLEY IS FULL OF PEOPLE WHO ARE ITCHING TO BE better than you. Dreamers who think one big idea will propel their careers. And in some ways, that's true. I moved there as a cocky 16-year-old who had a knack for hacking complex systems and needed to escape my shitty parents.

I couch surfed for a few months until I was brought into an app incubator. The next year of my life was spent living off ramen and energy drinks. Creating by night, sleeping a few hours here and there and bonding with the five other young developers like me. We wanted to make a difference in the world, finally use our skills for something good. Our idealism was through the roof. And we did. We created an app that helps connect people to community volunteer opportunities within a five-mile radius of where they lived. And we had so much fucking fun doing it.

The app sold for more money than any of us could've imagined. I took my share, and with some extra investor money started, Fox Enterprises. Getting people to take me seriously at 20 was hard at first. Shit, it was really hard. But ten years later we'd turned it into a billion-dollar company, disproving the early naysayers. They're the ones who begged for a way in once the company took off.

And now I need out. I'm restless. So, when the opportunity to sell presented itself, I grabbed on. Tired of the race to make more money.

I've forgotten why I loved technology to start with. I knew the foundation was the right direction the moment I started to dream it up. If I can help one kid who needs someone to believe in them, like I did, it'll be worth it.

I bought a house here and decided to spend some time away. I head back to the valley at the end of January. But lately, every day closer to going back makes this place feel more and more like home.

As soon as Jade left, I went to my office, forcing myself to work. I have a lot left to do to set up the foundation. I need something to take my mind off that kiss — Jade — all of it. Have I wanted to fuck her since I met her? Yes. Did I ever plan to? No. I have a strict no sex or relationships rule with anyone in my employ for a reason. *Been there, done that. Suffered the consequences.*

My rules went right out the window the minute she brushed her soft lips against mine. All I wanted to do was strip off every layer of clothing. Explore every dip and valley of her curves. The kind I can sink my fingers into, hold onto. Not to mention dark brown hair that I want to free from her prim little bun. And weave my hands through the strands - pulling, if she's into that kind of thing. And she is, my Jade doesn't know that I know. But tonight — I noticed her flushed face when I praised her.

Ending that kiss, acting like it meant nothing. Telling her she should leave? It was one of the hardest things I've ever done. The heartbreak on her face gutted me. *God, I'm such a dick.*

As though I summoned her, Jade's name flashes across my phone as it rings. When I hear her breathless and frantic voice replay the whole accident, I bolt out of my chair and race out to my Land Rover.

Now, just minutes after I swiftly navigated the freshly fucked up road from my house down the mountain, I find her 15-year-old silver rust bucket. Although I've teased her about this car before, there's nothing funny about the current situation.

Resting against trees, the front facing the wrong way, and a snow drift forming around the edges of the vehicle, I spot her standing beside it. Her arms wrapped around her middle, probably trying to hold in the warmth that this storm is leaching from her. Why isn't she inside with the heat running?

I park a foot away, jump out and stomp my way through the snow until she's right in front of me. She's staring forlornly at her car.

When I get to her, I can't help the need as I gently grip her arms, pulling her closer to my body and the heat that I'm desperate to share with her. "Jade, baby. Look at me." I tilt her chin up with one hand and she finally looks at me.

How fucking dare her. How could she put herself in danger like this. I was angry the first moment she murmured *car* and *trees*, but seeing her now, I'm livid. Seemingly unharmed should make me feel better but I'm somehow even more pissed.

If she notices me calling her baby, she must not mind because there's no reaction from her. Her cheeks are flushed a bright pink and her lips look red from where she's currently biting them. And the thing that guts me most is the sheen of tears in her eyes and the full body shivering she can't control. I tug my sweater off, over my head, and move to position it above her.

"Up," I say, nudging her hands and arms. She does as I say, obviously in a fog because this woman is never compliant. And that worries me. One of the things I love most about her is how brightly she burns. I pull my sweater down over her head - luckily, it's big enough to fit over her coat.

"Do you have everything you need from your car?"

"Yes. Oh, wait." She hurries to the trunk of the car, key in hand to unlock it.

She unlocks it and pushes it open with a creak, grabbing what looks to be a gym bag full of who knows what.

"This car should be in a junkyard." I can't help but spit out.

The red in her cheeks now is all anger. "Oh, excuse me! We can't all be rich assholes driving fancy cars they replace every two years." I know she's referring to the brand-new vehicle that she saw being delivered last week.

I can't help but grin. Riling her up is one of the few things that makes me smile.

Her brown eyes narrow at me, she marches up to me and pokes her finger into my chest. "How dare you. You think this is funny? I'll take my chances with a tow truck."

I know smiling at this moment is just making it worse. But I can't stop myself. "Not even a tow truck can get up here in this storm. Let me guess, you already called them and they said they can't make it for hours," I say smugly and cross my arms and lean against the hood of my car like I have all day. And I do. Because I know that she knows I'm right and at the end of the day, I'll get what I want. Which is her next to me in my car heading back to my house.

"Fine, I'll walk." She huffs and moves to pull my sweater up over her head, like she's going to return it and walk somewhere. Over my dead body.

I catch her with the sweater up over her face, tugging it back down into place, pulling her close. Her chest flush to mine. Jade lets out a little squeak at the contact. I know this is the wrong time for it, but all I want is for the clothes between us to disappear. To peel back the layers, she's wearing - the walls she's erecting as we speak.

I want to see her eyes hazy with lust.

"Here's what's going to happen. You're going to get into my car, and we're going back to the house. I'll make sure yours is towed as soon as that's an option." *To be used for scrap metal.*

The determination in her face falters a little, but I know she still wants to put up a fight, so I soften my approach. "You're going to freeze to death. The nearest home is a few miles away and you're not dressed for this weather. Which is another conversation we'll have when you're warm on the couch with a fire going."

"I can take care of myself. I'll figure it out."

"How's that going for you so far?"

"Ugh - the rumors are true. You really are a cold-hearted bastard."

I ignore her comment as she shoves away from me, slings her bag over her shoulder and stomps over to the passenger side of my car.

This snowstorm has been like some kind of late Christmas miracle. Fuck the rules. She doesn't know it yet, but she's mine. And I'm going to prove it to her.

5

Jade

Covertly, I look around Eli's car in awe once I'm seated. The cream leather interior is the softest thing I've ever felt. My car is so old, it only has a basic CD and cassette player. There's technology in this vehicle I wouldn't even know where to start with.

Trying not to let it make me feel inferior, but that's kinda tough when you're the personal assistant to a guy like Eli Fox. Everything about him screams confidence.

Opening up my *Why Jade Is Awesome* list in my head, I revisit exactly what makes me *not* inferior to Eli.

I'm a great friend.

I kick ass at my job.

I bake the best cookies and I'm a pretty talented writer. Though I waver on that last one, a lot.

Eli hops in on the driver's side, pressing a few buttons after turning on the car. Suddenly, I feel a welcome warmth under my ass. I can't help but let out a loud sigh. "I feel silly thinking heated seats are fancy when that's been around forever."

"Heated seats are a luxury I didn't know about until I was an adult. When I was a kid, growing up in Maine, it was so fucking cold. And we didn't always have money for heat.

When I went out on my own, I always swore I wouldn't be cold anymore." Eli says, looking over at me. A brief flash of pain crosses his face, one that he quickly masks.

That rare moment of vulnerability takes us both by surprise. I tuck a strand of hair behind my ear, anything to have something to do with my hands. I'm not used to this version of him. I know his background story, of course- everyone does. *Teenage genius comes to Silicon Valley and takes the tech world by storm.*

But I know nothing of his childhood, no one really does. It has always added an air of mystique to him. Like he just appeared out of thin air.

"Mine was the opposite. I grew up in a small coastal town in the south. It was always so freaking hot. We rarely had enough money for A/C. One of the things I love most about living here is that it's completely different than where I came from. Guess we have something in common."

His only response is a grunt in agreement.

"Why'd you buy a house here if you hate the cold?" I blurt it out before I can stop myself.

Eli's eyes crinkle at the corners, a genuine smile crossing his face. "Before I landed in California, I spent a season here, working in a ski shop. Slept on a buddy's couch. I learned to ski — realized I loved the freedom I felt on the slopes. I've come back here every year since and finally bought a place to have when I visit."

"I definitely never read that about you," I tease.

"No one really knows. I don't talk about a lot of my life before moving to the Valley," he says as we both sit in comfortable silence while we bump and roll over mounds of snow and ice in his SUV.

I place my hands under my thighs to keep them warm as I see the mahogany wood of Mountain Escape come into view. Of course it has a name, only wealthy people's homes have names.

The place suits him. With dark wood and giant glass windows highlighting the angles of the structure, it's a modern take on a rustic ski chalet. Throw in sky high Douglas firs surrounding the property, it looks like a holiday postcard carved into the mountains.

The outdoor fire pit is on a timer so it's already roaring to life. I've spent many evenings here over the last month helping with his foundation work. Oftentimes working around that pit.

I want nothing more than to run inside and find a hot shower. I hadn't realized how bone deep cold I was until now.

"Stay put." Eli gets out and quickly crosses around to my side, opening the door for me.

"Last I checked my legs aren't broken," I scoff.

"Shush," he says as he reaches in to lift me out like it's nothing.

Listen. I'm not ashamed of my curves. I grew up being told by my father that I couldn't be pretty without being thin. It took moving away, finding a new family in my friends here who are endlessly supportive, and a great therapist to learn and truly believe that's bullshit.

But that doesn't mean I'm light as a feather. And the way he picks me up with ease does something to my insides. It makes them feel all gooey and warm. Which is a problem, because he's still my client.

It doesn't help that he allows me to slowly slide down the front of his body before I settle on my feet again. I don't know where this version of Eli has come from. The hot to cold to hot again behavior, between last night and right now, is messing with my head.

We both trudge up to the massive front porch area, passing the handcrafted rocking chairs that surround the fire pit. Once he opens the etched glass door, I'm hit with a blast of warmth so amazing I almost whimper. The tingles in my feet and hands warn me that if I'd been outside any longer it'd have been a dangerous situation. Not that I plan to tell him he was right.

"Follow me," he instructs as we wind around the sunken living room filled with an oversized cream couch full of fluffy pillows and cozy throw blankets. Rounded out with a few plush chairs, a massive coffee table the main feature of the room, a stone fireplace that could heat the entire house I grew up in, it's truly gorgeous in here.

I can tell he's leading me to the wing with the guest suites. "I'm sure that I'll be able to get a tow truck up here soon. I can just thaw out a bit and then I'll be out of your hair. No need for me to have a room."

He halts so suddenly that I almost crash into his back. He turns and begins walking towards me, backing me up into the wall. Both hands go up on the wall, framing my head. "Let's get something straight. You're not going anywhere tonight. Probably not tomorrow either. This storm is due to last for the next two days. Do you actually think I'd allow you to risk your life by getting into a car with someone and trying to drive down this mountain?"

He's been closer to me twice in the last 24 hours than he has in the last 30 days, and it's like my brain completely malfunctions. All I can feel is the heat coming off his skin. I inhale the fresh pine, smoke and mint smell that is so uniquely him. There's no way he can't feel how hard my heart is beating. "It's - it's really none of your business. You're my client, not my boy—."

"Not what, Jade?" There's a dangerous glint in his eyes. The same one I saw earlier today, right before he kissed me back.

And I really need him to do it, but know that it can't happen again. I crossed the line and I know I need to somehow uncross it.

"Listen, that kiss this afternoon, I should never have done

that- it was completely inappropriate of me. You're one of ACS' most important clients and —. "

Eli emits a low growl. No, seriously an actual growl, "Like fuck it shouldn't have."

His smile is feral, and I'm starting to think he didn't regret anything about that kiss. But it's like he's also testing me - waiting to see what I'll do.

It makes me feel bold.

"You're not my boyfriend," I say, all the while shimming my body closer to him, pressing my breasts against his chest as he brings his hips to mine. I can feel the outline of his erection through the material of his jeans. Thank god for leggings, because it enables me to feel all of him. How long and thick he is. It takes all the willpower I have to stop from rubbing my core against him. I should be embarrassed that I'm this turned on from such little contact.

"Do you want me to touch you?" He whispers, gently tracing my neck with just a ghost of his lips.

"I, uh - we can't. Work. I'll get fired. Rules…." Damnit, I can't even get a complete sentence out, "and stuff."

"I've seen you work. You're the best damn employee they have. We're grown adults and I'm tired of denying myself what I want."

In the next moment the jarring sound of my phone ringing shatters the moment. I reach down to silence it, but fumble trying to find that right button. I yank it out and make the mistake of looking at who's calling.

Simon. Ugh. Freaking Simon. He never returns my calls in a timely fashion. Except this one time. The call ends before I can answer, only to start again immediately.

"Ignore it."

"I wish. He'll keep calling until I answer." I duck under Eli's arm and scurry into the living room. There's no way I can talk to my boss while dry humping our client.

Oh my god, what am I doing? I JUST RUBBED MYSELF UP AND DOWN MY BOSS' BODY.

"Simon, hi," I answer quickly, panting like I just ran a mile. *Ha! Me. Run. Hilarious.*

He wastes no time yelling at me through the phone, "What was this message about a car accident? I would hope you don't expect the company to cover the damages to your car."

No *how are you, Jade? Are you injured? Anything we can do since your car was most likely totaled?*

"I'm fine, Simon. But thank you for asking." I'm not normally so snappy, but between the accident and Eli, my emotions are all over the place. As well as my hormones. Definitely those.

Eli strides into the living room, making a beeline for me with a tense look in his eyes, holding out his hand, gesturing for me to give him my phone.

I cover the mouthpiece and whisper at him, "I got this. Seriously." He sighs, rolling his shoulders as he leans against the back of the couch. His hands gripping it tightly.

"Well, I assume you're home now. Just make sure you alert Mr. Fox that you won't be in on Monday."

"I'm on vacation all next week. Erm, you may have forgotten?"

"Hmm, that's right," Simon says gruffly, likely annoyed that I've reminded him about something he should already know. "Who approved it? Surely I didn't."

"Eli — er. Mr. Fox did, of course," I say, straightening to my full five foot four, hoping I can imbue confidence through the phone that way. I know he's about to ruin my time off.

"I would think taking an entire week off when their client has major deadlines in the next month isn't the action of someone who wants to be promoted. Who deserves it." His sneer comes through the phone loud and clear. "I think it might be time we reevaluate your employment status with the ACS. There's a lot of folks out there who want jobs…"

Ahhh, there it is. That manipulative bastard. I can feel the telltale signs of impending tears.

Eli lets out a muffled curse, "Oh, fuck this." Eli comes over and gently pulls the phone away from my ear, and I just let him — wait, what's he doing?

I reach to take it back, but he only shakes his head at me. "What are you doing?" I hiss.

Eli ignores me. "What the fuck did you just say to her," he snarls into the phone.

I can't hear Simon's response, but by the darkening expression on Eli's face, it wasn't the right thing to say.

"Don't bother trying to explain. Jade is here with me, where she'll stay until she can get home safely. Then she's going to take time off because she's been working herself to the bone meeting my demands. Last I checked, I'm the client — and Jade works with me. I'd advise you to be very careful not to piss me off. After all, you rely on clients like me."

Eli doesn't even have to yell. The low, even pitch of his voice carries the kind of command that anyone would drop everything to follow.

I have to admit, it's incredibly sexy.

I know I shouldn't love this, and I try to hide my grin by slapping my palm across my mouth, but it doesn't stop a snort of laughter from escaping me. No one ever talks to Simon this way. I'll probably still get fired once Eli is gone. But I'll deal with that when it comes.

Eli's eyes twinkle with a weird mix of anger and amusement as he winks at me before returning to business mode. Simon's frantic pleas and explanations are loud enough for me to catch a word here and there.

I would never. Please be reasonable.

I tune out whatever else is being said.

"See that it doesn't. I won't be so forgiving a second time," he says tersely, ending the call and tossing the phone onto the couch.

I'm sure there's hero worship mixed with lust in my eyes. "You really didn't need to do that."

Eli nods and crosses his arms, "Don't let anyone talk to you like that, Jade."

I snort in disbelief. "I don't —," but his look stops me mid-sentence. "What? I stand up for myself. You make it sound like I'm some sort of pushover! You don't even know me. I'm your assistant. Your temporary assistant at that."

He stalks closer to me, invading my space as I try to hold my ground, but can't help when I take a tiny step backwards.

I don't mind it though. Him. In my space.

It's like all my nervous energy amps up when he's in the room. And when he's just a hair's breadth away? My heart is pumping double time and I can't catch my breath.

"I know that when you're nervous you pull at the hem of your sleeves, usually the left one." He flicks his eyes down and sure enough, I'm tugging at the edges of my sweater, pulling at a loose thread coming free. On the left side, of course.

"Ha! big deal. Lots of people have nervous habits," I scoff and shove both hands behind me and take a giant step back, crossing my arms for good measure. See, I can be all cool and unaffected too.

He begins slowly walking towards me again, this time a very wicked look in his eyes.

"You put a horrifying amount of vanilla creamer in your coffee."

"Slanderous. It's the perfect amount."

"You're always checking on those around you. Even Simon - who deserves fuck all from you. But the chef, your friend, Katie. I hear you on the phone with her, encouraging her when her father tells her what a disappointment she is for not being a doctor."

"So I care about people. That's not a defining thing that

means you know me," I say throwing my hands up in frustration.

"You tried to convince the cleaning staff to take snacks home to their families. You are always after me to make sure I eat. Last I checked, that wasn't in your job description."

"You're making it sound like I'm some kind of nag or something. My job is to assist you. Making sure you remember to eat when you spend 12 hours a day in front of a computer is most likely in the damn job description!" I walk around him, just out of his reach and start fluffing the pillows on the couch.

"Know what I think?"

"You're constantly tidying up, doing things for others, making yourself useful so that you don't need to think about yourself."

"Oh, I'm sorry, are you suddenly a psychologist? Think I have abandonment issues?"

Maybe I do. Maybe I take care of everyone around me because it wasn't done for me.

"I know you better than you realize, Jade. You light up when you help me with the mentoring program. I don't know if you realize this, but when I first got here I didn't give a shit about anything anymore. Not the company. Not being on the board. Not even the foundation. You've breathed life into it for me again. I get to see it through your eyes and remember why I even started it."

All I can do is stare at him, seeing him as I never have before. His large hand cups the side of my neck, his thumb rubbing circles on my cheek. Heat in his eyes and a slight flush on his sharp cheekbones.

I'd like nothing more than to nuzzle into that hand. For him to pull me to him and make it easy to submit to him. Because I see it now. He wants me too. Knowing it's not one-sided is a heady feeling.

I'm clutching one of the pillows so tightly to my chest, as though that can keep my heart from falling out of my chest at his feet. I want to be brave and walk to him this time, throw my arms around his waist and kiss the hell out of him. But I won't. Because he's my boss, and he's not staying in Aspen. My heart's already broken at that thought - the deeper I get, the worse it'll be. Do I revel in what we could have for now and deal with the inevitable heartbreak?

Sensing my indecision, Eli sighs and slips his hands into his pockets. "I'm gonna go get cleaned up. Feel free to do the same. Your bathroom's fully stocked. Help yourself to anything in the house, the fridge — all of it. I'm going to do some work and then turn in early." He's back to his professional and strait-laced self. All the passion from before Simon's call feels like eons ago.

I've done nothing but push him away since he picked me up. But how the hell could I know he feels this way? I kissed him a few hours ago and he's the one who ran from it.

Without another word he strides out of the living room. Right before the hallway swallows him up whole, I call out to him. "Wait, um just one second."

For a second I almost think he'll keep going, but he stops and waits for me to say something. He's not going to make this easy for me.

"Thank you. For helping me, letting me stay here. I'll admit I can be a teensy bit stubborn, but yea — just thank you."

"That stubbornness, the fire, is one of my favorite things about you, Jade. Don't let anyone fuck with it," he says with a nod and continues on his way.

6

Jade

20 minutes later I'm neck deep in the oversized bathtub. I lit a few candles that were already in here and dimmed the lighting, leaving a soft glow from the chandelier. That's right, a motherfreaking chandelier in the bathroom. I can't even imagine what the ensuite in Eli's room is like if this is just the guest room.

The minute I walked into the bathroom I knew I'd never want to leave this place. Compared to my tiny one at home, with room only for a stand-up shower, toilet and pedestal sink, this one is both bright and open while warm and cozy at the same time. Just like everything in this house. The dark gray granite countertop is offset with chrome fixtures and a sunken sink, surrounded by a walk-in shower with not one but two rain shower heads. There's so much space that there's even a wide bench in the shower.

All I could think about when I saw it is me sprawled across it with Eli down on his knees in front of me.

Danger, danger. Stop those thoughts right now, ma'am. Think about anything else, Jade.

I lean my head back and close my eyes, letting my arms float out to my sides. Holy shit this is relaxing. I wonder what

Eli's doing. Is he thinking about earlier today? I can't seem to stop myself from replaying that kiss, then the moment in the hallway, in my head. The first time Eli bailed and then I did.

What would it be like if we both just gave in?

The image of Eli on his knees in front of me appears in my mind, front and center again, and this time I don't try to fight to keep the thoughts away. I continue to keep my eyes closed as I slowly slide my hand over the slope of my breast, dreaming about Eli putting both hands on my knees to push my legs apart. He stares down at me, swatting my hands away that instinctively move to cover myself. Slowly I slide my hand down my stomach, under the water until I meet the slick desire at my core.

I imagine him leaning down and flicking his tongue gently against my clit, while my fingers rub it in small circles. I dip my other hand under the water and push a finger inside. Thrusting and flicking in rhythm, picking up speed as molten tingles erupt across my skin. My core pulses, gripping my finger but needing more than this. All the while imagining that it's Eli's tongue dancing across the small bundle of nerves, his fingers rubbing in just the right spot deep inside me. Everything aches - I feel full but it's not enough. Dream Eli adds a second finger inside me, so I do the same, fucking my own hand, chasing an orgasm that's just out of reach. Water has been sloshing over the edge of the tub and I know I should care but I don't.

"Ah fuck, Eli." I can't stop myself from calling out. "Oh my god, yes. I'm gonna come." Just a little bit more, I press my finger a little bit harder, rubbing faster until I can feel the inside of my pussy clamp around my fingers, all the nerve endings in my body stand on end as my orgasm crashes over me.

7

Eli

THE FIRST THING I DID WHEN I GOT TO MY OFFICE WAS FIRE off a text to my business partner, Jake. We met when I first moved to Silicon Valley, he's the closest thing I have to a best friend, and is an extremely talented hacker, like me. I know he can find anything I ask quickly. And I want him to find out everything he can about Jade's asshole of a boss, Simon Lewis.

For the last hour, I've been staring at an email my lawyer sent me. I should be responding to it. Instead, I'm dealing with a throbbing erection caused by memories of the breathy moans Jade made as I kissed her. The way she tilted her head up to me, welcoming the crashing of our lips. Her soft hands reaching under my shirt and sinking her fingers into the muscles of my back.

Fuck it. I lean back in my swivel chair, quickly unbuttoning my jeans, my dick popping out in relief of being contained. If her asshole of a boss hadn't called her and interrupted us in the hallway earlier, I would've gotten her to admit that she wants this. Me.

I grip my cock in a tightened fist, spreading the pre-cum around for lubrication. It's a sorry excuse for her mouth but it'll do. God, what I wouldn't give to have her on her knees in here right now as I feed my length into her mouth. Licking and sucking. Her smaller hands gripping me tightly as she takes me as far as she can - till I hit the back of her throat and still ask for more. The tingle at the base of my spine lets me know I'm almost there and I begin jerking my hand harder and faster.

"Fuck, yes. Fuck me," I grunt as the release hits me, ropes of come painting my lower abdomen.

Instead of relaxed, I only feel more tense. That might've provided a little bit of relief, but it wasn't enough, it wasn't Jade. I don't know how we'll co-exist waiting out the storm now that we've opened Pandora's box.

8

Jade

I LAY BACK, EYES STILL CLOSED, TRYING TO CATCH MY BREATH. I can't believe I did that. I mean, sure maybe I've gotten off a time or 20 to fantasies of Eli. Ok - fine, he's been a regular feature in them more nights than I'd like to count since meeting him.

There's a chill in the air now that the bathwater has cooled. When I finally open them and look around, I see how much water has spilled out. I scramble out and gather all the extra towels I can grab and sop up the water.

Holy shit! I just got myself off while fantasizing about my boss going down on me. When he's right down the hall.

How can I face him? I called out his name! Did he hear me?

Ugh — as hungry as I am there's *no way* I'm leaving this room tonight. When I check the time on my phone I see it's 8:30 pm. Yep, perfectly normal time to go to bed. I need to fill the time until I can fall asleep somehow. I explore the drawers in the bathroom and see that Eli wasn't kidding about it being fully stocked. I find an extra toothbrush and luxury skincare products, brands I can't even pronounce. My skin feels brand fucking new once I'm done.

I bury myself in the silky-smooth sheets and cozy comforter on the queen bed and turn on the TV, hoping that something, anything will catch my attention and allow me to drift off to sleep.

Eli had the house professionally decorated for Christmas, so of course this room has its own tree, but I kind of love it.

With the lights out, and only the glow from the strands on the tree and the tv, I watch the snow fall outside the windows and drift off to a deep sleep of *Eli-Fox-filled-dreams*.

9

Jade

THE SMELL OF SUGAR COOKIES PULLS ME OUT OF SLEEP. I tossed and turned a bit throughout the night, each time waking up from a dream featuring me and Eli. The last one was the two of us, like together, together. Living here in this house, in a relationship. It freaked me out because it felt so real. So of course, it took forever to fall asleep again.

But it's that sugary sweet scent that finally makes me eager to get up and investigate.

Before heading to the kitchen, I grab the gym bag I grabbed from my car. The planner in me keeps it in my trunk with a few essentials like panties, yoga pants and a tank top. A shiver runs through me when I realize I don't have a sweatshirt or fuzzy socks, and I make a mental note to add warmer clothes to it.

Once I open the door and venture out, I'm hit with the coziest holiday feels. The fireplace in the living room is lit and giving off a delicious warmth my chilled skin needs. Eli has music piping out of one of the many wireless devices in this house. Christmas music, which I love. I'm a firm believer that all things Christmas can stay until after New Year's.

Outside the massive windows the snow is still falling, albeit at a lazy pace. The several inches that fell overnight are piled up on the ground and weighing down the tree branches. Icicles in various shapes and sizes hang down, completing the overall effect.

It's a flippin' winter wonderland. I love it so much.

The open concept floor plan allows me to see Eli as he's deep in concentration in the kitchen. A rolling pin in one hand as he takes a sip from the coffee mug with the other. The giant mug somehow looks tiny in his large, tanned hand. Even from here I can see his Adam's apple moving up and down as he swallows it. I catch myself staring, lusting after the one man I have no business being involved with. I give myself a mental shake and lock those thoughts and feelings away.

When I get closer, I take a closer look at the mug and see it features an illustrated gingerbread man on it with his hand broken off and the phrase, *Oh Snap* next to it. The giggle that escapes my lips has Eli looking up at me and grinning. He looks light and happy. I feel like I'm seeing a version of Eli very few have access to.

He spreads his arms out, gesturing to the dough and cookie cutters laid out on the kitchen island. "I thought we could bake cookies. If you want to, of course?"

Be still my heart. I usually bake holiday cookies alone since Katie is always working. It's an activity that brings back the best memories of doing all the Christmas things with my mom. I've always wanted someone to share that with, so yes, I sure as hell do.

I have to stop myself from bounding over to him like an excited puppy, "Got an apron?"

An hour later, we're both wearing ridiculous Santa aprons and putting the last batch of cookies into the oven and I'm schooling Eli in the fine art of flooding the cookies with icing. I take a mental snapshot of this big, strong brilliant man, bent over a tree shaped cookie as he tries to delicately apply pressure to the bag and fill in the outline.

"I didn't realize you were so into the holidays," I prod, wanting to know more about him.

He looks at me sheepishly. "My parents weren't around much — it wasn't a great situation, and that's why I left home at 16. We never celebrated holidays or birthdays or anything like that when I was growing up," he admits as he self-consciously runs his hand through his hair. "After I started making my own money and had my own place, I started my own traditions. Pun filled apparel and all," he laughs gesturing to his mug and apron.

"You seem to be a serious cookie expert..." he trails off waiting for me to share, which is only fair.

"I was an only child growing up, and my mom was a huge fan of the holidays. We're talking over the top decorations, baking and singing carols at home. Even without a lot of money, she always made the holidays feel special. And she taught me everything I know about cookies, and I like carrying on those traditions." I hesitate if I should share more, but I find myself wanting him to know me. "She passed away when I was 12. My dad was pretty broken by it, and then he remarried a year later. Things were never really the same after that," I say. I look down and sniffle a little, trying to keep the unexpected tears at bay.

Eli pulls me into his arms, tucking my head against his broad chest. "I'm sorry, I don't know why I'm being emotional. This is embarrassing," I whisper.

"Baby, you don't ever have to apologize to me for how you feel. The holidays bring up lots of emotions for people," he says gruffly while lazily running his hand up and down my back.

I know it's meant to be soothing. And it is. But I can't stop the goosebumps that break out all over my skin nor the fire that ignites in my belly.

Did he call me baby? He definitely did and I kind of love it.

"Eli?"

"Hmm?" He says as I look up at him, pulling away a little bit.

"What are we doing," I ask, pointing between the two of us. "What is this? I mean — there was yesterday, the kiss and then you pulled away. Then uh, the hallways," I mumble awkwardly, pulling away and moving to the safety of the other side of the island.

10

Eli

"What are we doing," Jade's question bounces around my brain — I stare at her as she keeps talking and puts distance between us.

Do I put it all out there? Admit my feelings for her? I'm pretty sure if I lay it all out there, she might run. She's been so set on maintaining our boss/employee relationship, but we're so far past that.

"I like spending time with you, Jade. You're intelligent and funny —."

"I wasn't fishing for compliments," she interjects sheepishly, but I hold my hand up to pause her from saying more.

"And so fucking beautiful it hurts to look at you. I've wanted you since the moment I met you."

And I want to paint your body with this icing and then lick it off. But I don't say that. She's too skittish, I need to work my way up to that.

A red flush has climbed up her chest and throat and all along her cheeks. "Oh, well. Right back atcha," she admits with a wink and a finger gun, immediately turning a deeper shade of red. She's fussing with her wrist like she's looking for a sleeve to unravel.

A grin breaks out on my face as I slowly stalk around the island to her.

11

Jade

"Right back atcha," I reply and immediately wish I could cram those words right back in my mouth. Better yet, I should stuff a cookie in my mouth so I stop talking. Here Eli is giving me these beautiful words. The kind I've only fantasized about and I'm acting like an awkward teenager.

Get it together, Jade.

I'm just staring, dumbfounded at him as he closes the distance between us, wearing that sexy smirk I've grown to love in the last 24 hours.

He reaches out to cup the side of my face, stroking a thumb against my cheek and leans down to whisper in my ear, "I want to explore this. Us."

"I would like that, uh, too," I stutter out. "But what about my contract? And you'll go back home at the end of January and —."

"Jade," Eli's voice is almost stern, which sends a whole other kind of shiver down my spine.

"Let's just live in the here and now. We're consenting adults. Contracts be damned. I'm not going to fire you. But if you're not comfortable with this, I understand, and it'll go no further. You're in charge here," he says as he backs away, shoving both his hands into the pockets of sweatpants.

For once, I think I'm ready to take what I want. I'm not normally a rule breaker, but this experience will be worth it. Come what may.

"I want this too," I say, moving to him quickly and pulling him down to meet my lips. No hesitation this time.

His lips crash onto mine and the kiss turns ravenous. Just like yesterday. Eli reaches down and picks me up and I wrap my legs around his waist, pressing my core against the ripples of his abdomen, I can feel every delineation through his thin t-shirt. His lips eat at mine, seeking entrance as one of his hands thrusts into my hair, gripping it tightly, pulling on it a bit, causing me to writhe against him.

In the distance I hear a beeping noise. Something trying to break through this moment. But I don't want anything to mess up this moment.

Eli's gripping one of the globes of my ass in his other hand, squeezing. The tiny bit of pain only amps up my arousal.

He pulls away slightly to look at me, his eyes hooded and intensely focused on me. I can see the desire in them. His hair is all mussed and his cheeks are ruddy. He's never looked hotter. We both just stare for a moment until that same beeping sound starts again and the faint smell of burnt sugar reaches my nose.

"Oh shit! The cookies." I shriek as Eli gently lets me down. I run to the oven turning off the timer we both ignored way too long. "Looks like this last batch is toasted," I say, pulling them out.

"Worth it," Eli says with a chuckle. "We've got plenty that turned out perfectly."

"So uh, what should we do now?" Eli's grin turns devilish at my question, and I swat him with the oven mitt, "I didn't mean *that*." But I did mean *that*. I need a few to get myself together. I could so easily get carried away and lost in him, in this perfect place.

"We're going on a date tonight," Eli declares, crossing his arms and leaning against the kitchen island, one foot crossed over the other like I can't see his raging and massive hard on through his pants. I'm trying desperately not to look.

"Ms. Williamson, are you staring at my cock?"

I'm pretty sure I could melt into the floor with embarrassment and that still wouldn't be enough.

Change the subject. Oh my god.

"Uh, we can't really go anywhere. In case you missed it, there's an epic amount of snow that has fallen."

"A date here. I'm cooking dinner for us. Then a movie, maybe some fireworks. It's New Year's Eve after all," Eli says. "Now let's finish these cookies. I've got a hot date tonight and need time to get ready."

12

Eli

WE SPENT THE NEXT FEW HOURS DECORATING COOKIES AND laughing. Exchanging lingering touches and looks. I've been turned on all day, but it's been worth it.

We've finally settled in the living room with steaming plates of pasta carbonara. When she told me her original New Year's Eve plans were pasta and wine, I knew immediately what to make us.

We talk about how much she loves to write and that her dream is to be an author. And how her ideal job would offer her the ability to write on the side. Her current one certainly doesn't. Simon's a fucking asshole and well, I'm a pretty demanding boss. It makes me really happy when she talks about how much she's enjoyed the foundation work. Hell, I couldn't ask for someone better than Jade working for it. I wonder if it's something she'd consider.

She tells me about growing up in South Carolina, how she couldn't wait to get out and travel, see other places. Be someone else than she was growing up. I tell her about growing up in that small Maine town. She listens to every word with rapt attention.

"I'm so sorry that you had a hard childhood. That your parents were so awful. "

"They were two people who should've never had a kid. And it's ok. I'm an adult now, and my life turned out pretty well despite that."

Jade reaches across the couch and takes my hand in hers, squeezing. "It did. But you still shouldn't have had to leave home at 16 to try and make it on your own in the world."

Suddenly she moves to get up and reaches for our plates.

"No, let me," I say as I put a halting hand on her arm, and don't say anything else as I grab our plates to put them in the sink, hoping to give myself a minute.

It's very rare that I talk about my past with anyone. Somehow in such a short time of knowing each other, Jade has managed to get under my skin. It feels uncomfortable but exhilarating. I've dated here and there over the years, but Fox Enterprises kept me so busy I didn't really have time for a relationship. I preferred to keep things casual, surface level. I rarely slept with the same woman twice.

Except one, Emily. She worked for my company. First, we were colleagues and friends, eventually becoming lovers. She's the only woman I've ever told that I loved them. It unfortunately blew up in my face when I found out she was screwing me over. It messed me up for a long time. And I never wanted to try again. Until now.

I pad back into the living room to find Jade flipping through channels.

"When I was a kid and my mom was still alive, we'd have movie night every New Year's Eve. We didn't have much money, so she was great about turning it into a whole celebration without having to spend a lot. We'd have popcorn, candy and so much soda I'd burst. Those are some of my favorite memories," she says, smiling up at me from her position on the couch. Her legs are crossed so her feet are tucked up under here.

She looks up at me excitedly. "So, what are we watching?"

I love seeing her like this. "You pick. I need to grab my sweatshirt."

I run back to my room to grab a sweatshirt. I check my phone on the nightstand and see a text message.

Jake: I found something, gimme a call when you can.

Most people outside the service and hospitality industry wouldn't be working at 9:30pm on New Year's Eve. But Jake's always working. And he knows if I ask for something urgent, it must be important.

I quickly call him, curious what he's found, knowing it must be something I can use if he's texting me about it now.

The ringing stops and his voicemail takes over. Ending the call, I tap out a text back.

Eli: Send it via email when you can. Thanks for the quick work. Enjoy the holiday, man.

I grab two sweatshirts and come back to the room to find the couch empty.

"Yesssss!" I hear an excited squeal as Jade prances back into the living room with two large bowls of freshly popped popcorn along with her bottle of wine and my bourbon. "I'm so glad you have popcorn here. It's not a movie night without it."

"I don't remember the last time I had a movie night. Maybe never?" I say — hoping this is the start of a new tradition.

"Prepare to have your life changed. Now, for the movies. Feeling like a classic or something new?" Seeing this side of her - this carefree and adorable, is like a breath of fresh air.

I hand her the extra sweatshirt. She puts it on, and it hangs down past her ass. The sleeves swallow her whole. Something primitive in me loves seeing my clothes on her.

I sit back down on the couch and prop my feet up on the coffee table. I crook my finger at her. "C'mere."

She smiles shyly and scoots over, but not quite close enough.

"God, you're fucking adorable." I lean over and put one hand behind her back and one under her ass and pull her to me so our sides are lined up. She snuggles into me and I drape my arm around her. As I lean down and place a kiss on the top of her head, her unique scent of vanilla and spice fills my nose. She smells like a goddamned sugar cookie in the best possible way.

And to think I was going to spend New Year's Eve alone. There's nowhere else I'd rather be than here with her.

13

Jade

Spending the last two hours snuggled up with Eli has been pure magic. I picked a romcom and we spent the majority of it cracking jokes about how awful it was. The actors did their best, but the dialogue was ridiculous, as well as the plot, but that somehow made it even more fun.

I knew Eli had a dry sense of humor that I've always appreciated. But hearing him laugh and seeing him smile tonight? If I wasn't already in love with him, I would be now.

Not to mention he's spent the last few hours stroking his fingers along my forearms and my hands. Between the tension of our encounters today and now this, every touch feels like a live wire.

I've turned the tv back to a national news station and they're covering the Times Square celebration. Ten minutes to midnight.

"If there was one moment you could do over this year, what would it be?"

Eli doesn't even take much time to think before answering. "Yesterday, when we kissed. I wish I hadn't pulled away."

"Haha, what? Out of your entire life, you regret *that*?"

"Yes. Because out of every experience I've had this year,

hell the last several years, being here with you has been my favorite."

Before I can respond, he tilts my head up by my chin, and our lips crash together. He easily dominates me, and I submit because it's so easy to do with him.

"Put your arms around my neck," he instructs between kisses. Then Eli maneuvers us so that he's able to stand up, both hands securely under my thighs lifting me with ease.

"Oh my god, no. I'm too heavy."

"Baby girl, you are not. I've got you." Something about those words brings the bite of tears to my eyes. Very few people in my life have truly *gotten me*. Except for Katie and our small group of friends here. But past boyfriends have not.

I begin trailing kisses down his neck, sucking lightly as I move. He slowly releases my thighs and lets me gently slide down his front until I'm back on my feet again.

He keeps his head close to mine and whispers, "Undress for me. Let me watch," as he backs up and sits back down, his legs spread as he grabs his drink and takes a sip, watching me with a gleam in his eye. I've never done this before, but I want him so bad I'm not going to even think about being embarrassed.

I pull the sweatshirt he gave me off first, then my yoga pants. Lastly, I move to my bra and release the clasps. My breasts are aching and heavy when released from the cups. I stop for a moment, just breathing. Reveling in the look on Eli's face. His pupils widened as I take each piece of clothing off until I'm just down to my panties.

"Jesus, baby," Eli growls as he leans forward and stops my hands from grabbing the sides.

"Leave them on for now. I want to imagine how wet you're getting them right. Are you soaked for me, fucking dripping down your thighs?" Eli slides off the couch onto his knees in front of me.

"Sit," he commands.

I don't even think, I move back and sit on the couch. In just my panties. This feels both thrilling and naughty.

In the background I hear the tv host, "Four minutes till midnight. Make sure to pop those mints and find your New Year's Eve kiss!"

"Mmm, think I can make you come right as we hit midnight?" Eli's gruff voice skates across my skin, causing goosebumps to erupt all over. A shiver runs through me.

Eli sits back on his heels, both hands on my knees pushing them as wide as they can go. I'm incredibly exposed and I instinctively move to close them, cover myself. "Hey, hey. It's ok if you don't want me to do this," Eli says, concern in his eyes.

"It's not that - uh, oh god this is embarrassing. And I'm ruining the moment." I put both hands over my eyes.

Eli gently pulls my hands from my eyes. "I want you, in every way. But I won't do anything you're uncomfortable with. Talk to me, Jade."

How do I explain to this man in front me that my last boyfriend told me he didn't like going down on me. That it just wasn't for him. In fact, he didn't like a lot of things about me, and he made sure to tell me how inadequate he found me, physically and sexually.

I close my eyes, unable to face him as I say the words. "I just haven't had great experiences with it. My last boyfriend, well he didn't like doing it. And now that it's been a few years since we were together, I can see that it wasn't a me thing, but I haven't been with anyone since. Those same insecurities are still there I guess."

I know my face is flushed red with the old feelings of shame that resurface.

"Open your eyes, Jade," Eli says almost angrily. I meet his eyes and am fixated by his fierce expression. "That guy was a fucking idiot. I want to explore every single part of your body. Find all the spots that drive you wild. From your pussy and tits to your ass. I want it all. Please, let me erase that piece of shit from your memory."

I let out a shuttered breath. "Yes. Please."

"Good girl," he praises.

I never thought those two words would be my thing. New kink unlocked. I can't wait to see what others I might discover with Eli. Even if we only have this weekend, I'm going to let myself enjoy this.

Eli bites down on my inner thigh just enough to cause a pinch and send another bolt of lightning to my core. He continues kissing his way up one thigh, then the other. Each time he'd pass his lips and tongue gently across my clit, the tiny bundle of nerves only getting a taste to keep me on edge, and then kissing the seam of my panties.

Eli takes a deep breath. "You smell so fucking good. Do you think you taste even better?" He says looking up from between my thighs, his eyes hooded, and nostrils flared just a bit like he's inhaling my scent.

I should be embarrassed. In the past, sex has always lasted just a few minutes, two positions max and a somewhat clinical choreography. As though we each followed a script. Kiss here, suck there. Rub, rub, pump, pump. Done.

But this? The feral look in his eyes like he's seconds away from devouring me. I want to keep him on edge, just like he's doing to me.

I don't know where this version of me comes from, but I hold out my hand, right in front of his face. "Here's your taste," I tease, nudging my finger gently at his lips, seeking entry. Something about this moment, the way Eli's looking at me — I wish I could draw so I could capture this moment. I never realized how heady a feeling it is to be wanted, especially by this man.

I expected him to be frustrated, instead he appears amused as he sucks the finger into his mouth, biting down gently before releasing it with a pop.

"Such a good little tease," he says, suddenly gripping one side of my lacy panties. One sharp tug and the fragile lace tears. Then the other side. Eli peels the fabric away. I'm completely exposed to him, in more ways than one.

It's the only pair of underwear I have with me, but I'll worry about that later.

"Look at this pretty pussy," he growls as he slides one finger over my slit, unveiling my clit. He dips a finger low and drags it back up, swirling the wetness of my own arousal against the sensitive nerves. Eli's dirty talk already blows the other guys I've been with, all four of them, out of the water.

I feel like I should be shocked, but instead I let the words of praise wash over me, preening a bit. Then two fingers plunge inside, while his thumb continues to rub lazy circles.

The walls of my pussy clench around his fingers, desperately trying to hold onto them every time he draws them out to the very tip, only to pump them quickly back in again. He hooks both fingers inside, a come-hither motion that thrums the ridges of my G-spot. The thumb on my clit is replaced by his tongue.

What starts out as short laps and long licks from his fingers and back to my clit again, turns into a fast flicker as he flutters his tongue against. I can't help but reach down, grabbing his hair and pulling his face closer, burying it as I ride his face.

The vibration of his chuckle almost sends me off as he backs down a bit, causing me to whine at the loss of pressure. "You are such a greedy thing, aren't you? Mmmm," he says as he licks his lips.

"Oh my god. I'm so close, please, please don't fucking stop." I can barely control my breathing or my body — it's trembling all over.

"Eyes on me," the command is clear and strong.

I force my half-shut eyes open, my vision hazy as I'm lost in a pre-orgasmic dream. Keeping eye contact he descends again thrusting a third finger inside as well as he sucks my clit into his mouth only to continue torturing it with his tongue and the suction of his mouth. I'm unconsciously thrusting myself onto his fingers, pushing myself further into his mouth.

"Fuck my hand baby, god yes. Do you know how goddamn beautiful you are right now?"

"I'm gonna come, oh my god. Yes, please Eli!"

"Come for me baby. Soak me with it. You're such a good fucking girl."

Between his words, hand and that dirty mouth, I detonate. I can hear fireworks in the distance. My entire body is a live wire — pulsing with the pleasure running through it.

He continues to gently lap at my pussy, his fingers still working me inside, slowly rubbing as intense aftershocks ripple through me. My body jerking involuntarily from how sensitive my entire core is right now, but even that won't get me to make him stop. I come back to myself and realize that the fireworks I hear are going off outside, probably from down in the village and on the TV.

"How do you feel, beautiful?" Eli grins at me, his lips and chin shiny from me. Oh my god.

"Ummm —" I can't think straight. Can you be drunk off an orgasm? "That was amazing."

Eli reaches down and pulls me up with both hands and then sweeps me up in his arms and stalks off down the hallway.

"Ahhh, what are you — where are we going?"

Eli stops walking and looks down at me as I hold on around his neck for dear life.

"I want you in my bed. I want to fuck you. We've got all night. Yes or no, Jade?" The look on his face is serious and I know my answer means either a night of unspeakable pleasure or that I go back to my room alone.

"Yes, Eli. Yes." And that's all he needs before he carries me off and swings his bedroom door shut behind us.

14

Eli

"Yes, Eli. Yes." The three most beautiful words I've ever heard. I can't get us to my room fast enough. When I do, I release her onto the bed. She bounces as she lands, her tits bounce as well. She leans back on her elbows, unknowingly thrusting her chest up towards me. Her nipples begging for my mouth.

I quickly shove my sweats and black boxer briefs off and then tug my sweatshirt off with one hand and immediately crawl up the bed to Jade. She drops her knees open as though to welcome me in.

Her pink pussy glistens, wet from my mouth and her orgasm. The only light in the room is the warm glow from the bedside lamp and the full moon.

I place small kisses on her belly, leading up to her breasts. Sucking one puckered nipple into my mouth while my fingers play with the other. Pulling and tweaking. Jade's making tiny whimpers of pleasure, her body undulating uncontrollably.

"Tell me what you want," I command as I release her nipple with a pop.

"I — I uh,"

"Words, Jade. I need your words."

"I want you, Eli. Please."

"Please what? Where do you want me, Jade?" I murmur, drifting a hand down to her slit, dragging my fingers through her drenched pussy up to her clit. Softly rubbing because I know how sensitive she must be.

"OH!" she gasps and quickly closes her thighs around my hand, gripping it to keep me locked in place.

Her eyes have drifted closed.

"Open your eyes." Her eyes open revealing desire swimming in her deep brown eyes. The gold stands out, shimmering.

I sit up on my knees, on either side of her hips and grip my cock, stroking it up and down. Jade can't stop herself from staring at it raptly as she reaches her hand out to stroke it with me. Circling the head, drops of pre-cum coating her fingers as she pushes my hand away and takes over.

She stares at me, at it in fascination. The confidence in her eyes only turns me on more as her strokes go from hesitant to assured. The bottom of her lip is gripped between her teeth as she concentrates on her task. It's the hottest fucking thing I've ever seen.

"Baby, stop." She jerks her hand away, hurt entering her eyes, "Not like that. I'm about to explode, but I need to be inside you when I do."

15

Jade

I'm not ashamed to admit I'm panting from Eli's ministration. I feel like I could come again and he's not even inside me yet.

His cock juts out proudly, bobbing up towards his abs, cut with muscles and the deep vee that points at his dick like some sort of arrow. He's sitting on his knees on either side of my hips and is slowly rubbing his hand up and down the impressively thick and long length. His huge hand swallows it and reveals it as the muscles in his forearm up to his bicep ripple and flex.

I'm not sure how it's going to fit, but I can't wait to try. I reach up with my hand and tentatively begin rubbing the large head, almost purple in color he's so hard. A rush of heat runs through me, I can feel my own arousal leaking out, more than ready to accept him.

My confidence grows as his eyes drift shut with the movement of my hand, and I shove his out of the way as I take over.

Eli lets out a low groan, "Baby, stop." I pull my hand away like his dick is on fire. "Not like that. I'm about to explode but

I need to be inside you when I do," he says as his eyes meet mine.

"I want you inside me, now," I whisper.

He crawls off me and reaches into the nightstand to pull out a couple condom packets. He quickly unwraps one and rolls it down his length. He even makes that hot somehow.

Watching him touch himself while he's above me feels heady. Like I'm at his mercy, but in a way that I want to be.

He repositions himself between my thighs. "Hands," he commands as he taps the space above my head. I move them both up and he locks them both together in one hand while his other reaches down under my hips, hauling me up so that he can line his cock up with my slit. The first nudge of his head, the slight stretch hurts so fucking good, I let out a sigh.

"More," I moan as he slowly feeds his cock into me. Slowly in an inch, out a bit, in another inch, out a bit. Until finally I can't handle the teasing.

"Fuck me, Eli. Please god fuck me."

In one thrust he's fully seated. The fit is tight, almost too tight, but it's a delicious kind of pain. He holds there as his eyes meet mine. Letting me adjust to him.

"You ok?" He asks.

"Yes, better than ok. Please, don't stop." I nod in confirmation.

"You're all mine now baby," he says as begins thrusting, slowly at first — careful to watch me for signs of discomfort. He leans down to kiss me, nibbling at my bottom lip and then nipping it. At my whimper he leans back with a wicked smirk on his face.

"You feel so fucking good." Thrust. "Whose pussy is this?" he asks as he slows his thrusts and releases my wrists to move his hand, to begin playing with my clit. Flicking in time to his cock moving in and out of me.

My eyes close as my back bows, the pleasure is so intense. But he's keeping me on the edge. Every time I feel like I'm going to explode, he slows back down, withholding it just a little bit. By the smile on his face, he knows what he's doing.

"Please, Eli. I need to come," I beg. I'm not above begging at the moment. I'd do anything to make this last, but that pinnacle is just out of reach, and I need it desperately.

Eli's muscular chest glistens from the effort, I know he's just as affected as I am. The veins in his neck stand out as he controls himself.

"Answer my question. And maybe I'll let you come," he grits out. His jaw is granite hard, and his lips are pressed in a tight line as he watches me.

"You. It belongs to you," I shout, unable to stop the words from tumbling out. Not wanting to stop them, because it feels right. I'm his. For now, at least. Just as he is mine.

The wicked smirk is back as he lifts one of my legs up over his shoulder and leans down over me and begins thrusting faster and harder. His fingers continue to rub my clit, and it's too much.

"That's right baby. Come for me. Soak my dick," he grunts in my ear as I tip over the edge, coming as the pleasure rolls over me in waves. It feels like my whole body is vibrating and on fire.

The warm gush of orgasm means I'm even wetter as he moves in and out faster, harder.

"Fuck yes. Goddamn, I'm coming baby," Eli says as I can feel him pulse inside me. His thrusts slow, and gently he rides me through the rest of his orgasm.

I hold onto him tight as he presses kisses across my cheeks and forehead, before our lips meet in slow lingering kisses. My arms wrap around him and hold on tight. I don't want this moment to end. I don't want our snow globe to burst. Tears dot my eyes as I think about the possibility of him leaving soon.

I'm so fucked.

16

Jade

I WAKE UP TO A WARM HAND STROKING UP AND DOWN MY BACK. "Mmmm, that feels good," I muffle into the very hard pillow I'm currently resting my head on.

Hard pillow? Pillows don't feel like sleek muscles encased in smooth skin last time I checked. My pillow chuckles, a warm sound that sends an ache straight through to my core. I pop my eyes open. And meet Eli's emerald green eyes, as he peers down at me, amusement in his gaze.

His dark wavy hair is tousled and sticking up in some places. The grin he wears is both wicked and carefree. This is the most relaxed I've ever seen him, and it makes me feel all warm and fuzzy inside to think that I'm part of the reason why.

"Morning, beautiful," he says as I surreptitiously look to make sure I haven't been drooling on him. I wipe the sides of my mouth for good measure.

The previous night comes screaming back. The reminders of all the ways Eli worshiped my body can be felt the minute I move to sit up. Sore, but in the best way possible.

Spending the night with someone for the first time always

feels awkward. Do I stay? Do I...go to my room? First things first. I desperately have to pee, but the thought of getting out of this bed in the stark daylight, naked, all my flaws on display, is kind of terrifying.

Sensing my discomfort, Eli leans over and drops kisses along the top of my shoulder as he draws his lips up the side of neck. All the awkwardness fades as my body begins to melt back into him.

"I'm going to go make us some coffee," he says. And thank goodness because my bladder was about to protest me ignoring it.

Not lacking any confidence, Eli flips the covers back, climbing out of bed. I can't help but admire him as he walks to the dresser. Every bit of his body is sculpted muscle. From his calves up to his thighs that could crack walnuts. The sleek muscles of his back ripple as he walks, each delineation clear. And everything converges to a round, full and sculpted ass. I never would've thought a guy who sits behind a computer all day could look like this.

He pulls out a pair of - you guessed it, gray sweatpants. Does he own a pair for each day of the week? I'm not complaining of course - though I do want to whine as he slides them up covering his firm cheeks. He turns around, the waistband riding low on his hips, not leaving anything to the imagination.

"Like what you see?" he says with a smirk.

"Oh my god, go!" I toss the pillow I'm holding at him, which he handily dodges, laughing as he walks out towards the kitchen.

I hurry out of the bed into the bathroom. My hair is a tangled mess. Definite bedhead. I realize I'm in his bathroom with no supplies to tame it. So, I quickly do my business, wash my hands and face and steal some of his mouthwash.

Damnit. I don't have anything to put on. I turn around the

bathroom, looking for something, anything. I don't even see a towel, until I spot the hook on the back of the door. One of Eli's t-shirts is hanging from it. Better than nothing. It falls just below the edge of my butt. I open the door and tiptoe out, unsure if Eli is back in the bedroom yet.

Where the hell are my panties? They're not on the floor - oh crap! They're on the living room floor. In shreds since he tore them off me. I don't know why I'm being so shy around a man who explored every inch of my body last night.

Right at that moment Eli appears in the doorway, a tray in his hand with two mugs. Steam swirling up from the tops. The smell of dark roast and vanilla fills the room. I start to get up and help him, but he shakes his head.

"Back in bed." He sets the tray down and now I can see an array of the cookies we made yesterday.

When he hands me the mug, I take a deep sniff. It's the color caramel, just the right amount of cream has been added. I take a sip and it's the best coffee I've ever had. I can't stop the moan that escapes my lips. Eli is still standing on my side of the bed, staring at me with so much heat in his eyes.

"This is honestly the best cup of coffee I can remember having. How did you know to fix it just how I like it?"

"Because I've paid attention to you, Jade. Everything from how you take your coffee to the way you twist your lips when you're trying to solve a problem."

My next sip almost chokes me when he says, "Besides, I overheard you talking to Katie the other night. Something about sleeping in, a great cup of coffee and amazing sex. We slept in. And I'm pretty sure, by the number of times you called out my name last night..." He trails off with just a knowing look on his face.

The coughing starts before I can even spit the hot liquid out. Which prompts Eli to take the mug out of my hand with a laugh.

"C'mon, sweetheart. Take a shower with me," he says as he saunters towards the bathroom.

Once there, he wastes no time stripping the shirt up and over my head, leaving me naked. He follows suit, removing his sweatpants, his thick long cock is so hard, it's curved up towards his lower abdomen. The blast of hot water is a welcome shock to my sore muscles.

Eli pours shampoo into his hands. "Turn around," he commands.

As I present him with my back, he begins massaging the shampoo through my hair, taking his time, working it through every strand. He moves down to push his fingers into the base of my skull, rubbing my tired neck muscles and then further down to my shoulders. My head falls forward, a soft sigh escaping.

He maneuvers me under the spray rinsing my hair out.

I suds a cloth with his body wash and move it across his broad shoulders, down his biceps and the forearms that I can never stop staring at. I scrub across his chest and abdomen while he looks down at me silently.

His cock poking me in the belly - I reach down and give it a firm squeeze, prompting Eli to let out a soft grunt. I gently wash him there, exploring as I do.

I want him in my mouth, just thinking about it is making me wet. I don't have a ton of experience with blow jobs, but I want to do this for him, to make him feel even a fracture of the pleasure he's given me.

Rinsing the soap off of him, I lower myself to my knees. I take the base of him in my hand and look back up at him.

He's leaning over me, one hand on the wall behind me, as though he needs to be held up. I reach my tongue out and flick it against the opening at the tip of his dick, tasting his arousal. Salt and musk and very much him, I immediately want more. So, I close my lips around the head and slowly begin working him in and out of my mouth, using my hand as well.

"The image of you with my cock in your mouth is going to be the death of me," he says as he places his hand on the back of my head, gently thrusting as I swallow him whole.

"Challenge accepted," I say as I release him for a moment, grinning up at him.

17

Eli

After our shower I carried Jade to the bed, propping her on her hands and knees and fucking her hard, edging her until she begged me to let her come.

Afterwards she drifted off to sleep, so here I am in the kitchen writing her a note to tell her the roads have been plowed enough to get out and that I'll be back soon.

According to the news, the roads have been cleared enough to get around. Even though it's a holiday. That's the benefit to living in a place prepared for harsh winter weather. I wish we were still stuck here. That way She wouldn't have to go home, and we could keep living in this fantasy.

I've called a tow to have her car taken to the nearest body shop in town. As much as I wish she'd drive something else, I understand buying her a new car is a boundary she's not ready for me to cross. Her independence is one of the things I love about her.

Love.

That's right. I can finally admit that I'm in love with Jade. I never thought I'd fall prey to this emotion again. I've been fighting it all these months. Writing it off as admiration or just pure lust. But after last night I know it deep in my bones. I don't want to scare the shit out of her by telling her just yet.

I've been in love exactly one other time. And it didn't end well. It's why I swore off relationships five years ago. That relationship was hard. Way harder than it needed to be. We could never just be with each other.

Some of my favorite moments with Jade have been while we've worked together. Just giving each other shit - seeing how much she cares about what she does. She deserves this promotion. And fucking Simon better not ruin it for her.

I still haven't heard back from Jake, but I'll give him a call when I go into to town to see if he's got that update for me. If Jade wants her promotion, I'll damn well make sure she gets it. I won't let Simon ruin it. Even if I think she should pursue her dream. It's not up to me, but I'm more than happy to remove the barriers for her.

I stop by my room, peering inside to see Jade passed out. Her dark hair spread all over her pillow, one leg hiked up hanging out of the sheets. I want this- her in my bed, our bed, every day. When I get back, I'll continue laying that groundwork.

18

Jade

I WAKE UP TO MY PHONE RINGING OVER AND OVER AGAIN. THIS time there's no Eli in bed with me. He must be in his office working. The memories from last night and this morning make me blush as I recall each moment, each kiss, every dirty word. Oh my god — it was the hottest experience of my life.

I can't fall down this rabbit hole. I get up, walking towards Eli's dresser and snag a pair of his sweats and a t-shirt. It all smells like him and feels like I'm wrapped up in his arms. With that happy thought I toss my hair up into a sloppy bun.

Suddenly my stomach grumbles loudly, and I realize I haven't eaten anything other than that cookie with my coffee, four hours ago. I grab my phone and make my way to the kitchen. Checking my messages as I go.

Two texts from Katie, just wishing me a happy new year followed by several eggplant emojis. My only reply is a bunch of kissy faces.

Three missed calls from Simon. THREE. "What the hell?" I really don't want to call him back. I worked yesterday when I wasn't supposed to. And I'm finally going to put my foot down. So no, I won't return his call on my day off. It's also a freaking holiday! He can wait.

Feeling proud of myself for finally setting a boundary, and following it, I take out all the items I need to make omelets for us both.

I take off for Eli's office to ask him what he wants in his eggs. Right as I pass the front hallway the doorbell rings. Weird timing.

I go to take a peek outside. "Oh shit." It's Simon. I want to duck, but there's nowhere to hide. Plus, the door is just intricately carved glass. So even though I probably appear warped, there's no way he doesn't know it's me.

"Jade!" He calls out, ringing the bell again. Yep, he knows it's me.

I trudge to the door, my stomach sinking with every step. I don't even have time to give myself a once over. I'm not even wearing a bra. And with that thought I'm remembering that said bra and ripped panties are probably still lying on the living room floor. Proof of our night together visible all over the place. *Shit.*

I crack the door open, hoping our entire interaction can be contained here.

"Happy New Year, Simon," I say awkwardly as I plaster a fake smile on my face.

"Jade, open the door," he says while pushing the door open, and me back. He walks in and turns around to face me. "Where's Fox?"

I don't know how Eli would feel about Simon using his last name as a casual nickname. Probably wouldn't, considering how much he dislikes him.

"I think he's in his office. I'll grab him," I say as I scurry over to the office door. Desperately hoping I can stay in there while he and Eli talk. Except when I step into the room, it's empty. It doesn't even look like he's been here today. Everything is too organized.

Crap, where is he? Why didn't he tell me he was going somewhere? This isn't great.

Do I go back out there to talk to Simon? I'm so mortified. Just because I can't stand him doesn't mean I don't have to respect him as my boss. And last I checked, chatting with your boss in your very fucking VIP client's home while wearing said client's clothing, and looking freshly fucked by said client, isn't a great plan.

Think, Jade. Think.

The unmistakable sound of Simon clearing his throat breaks through my panic. It's OK. Everything is fine. I double check my appearance in the mirror hanging behind a decorative desk.

Rat nest for hair. Check. Nipples at full attention and visible through the shirt. Check.

I quickly cross my arms and march myself back out there. I was just convincing myself not even 10 minutes ago that it's time I stopped letting him push me around.

I skirt around Simon, hoping to draw him to the kitchen, but he of course wanders to the living room. Please don't sit on that couch. Visions of Eli going down on me in that exact spot make my face flame.

I let out an audible sigh of relief when he keeps walking to stand at the wall of windows at the back of the house, stopping to admire the snow-covered trees.

"Quite a view here."

"Eli — er Mr. Fox obviously has excellent taste." Facepalm, Jade.

"You've been spending every day up here, holed up in this house. Just the two of you these last few months."

I narrow my eyes suspiciously. What's he getting at with this?

Simon appears nonchalant, but I've learned his tells. When he's getting ready to eviscerate someone, he puts his hands in his pockets. He leans against a wall. He doesn't want his victims to know he's a snake about to strike at any point.

"You see, I'm surprised, knowing how much you've

wanted this promotion, that you'd throw it all away by throwing yourself at our most important client."

Outrage. Fucking outrage. How dare he!

Instead of hand wringing and stilted answers, my voice is firm, the tone even when I respond, "I've been doing my job, Simon. And I think if you asked Mr. Fox, I've been doing it pretty damn well. I'm hoping I've proven how capable I am to take on the role as Director of Client Experience." Simon's eyes widen, clearly not used to me standing up to him.

Take that assface!

"Jade, Jade, Jade," he tisks. "What I'm observing is you, here in the home of your client. Disheveled. Things tossed about. No sign of Mr. Fox. Have you not paused to wonder where he is?"

"What —. "

"He called me first thing this morning. Let me know that he's decided to end his contract with us early."

"That's not possible. He's here another month."

"That may be, but he's asked that we find him someone else. He no longer wants your…services," Simon says with a leering sneer.

"I don't believe you."

"Did you really think that you two would just keep playing house? Up here in the lap of luxury? That maybe you'd somehow catch a man like Eli Fox?"

Yes. A tiny voice in my head whispers.

I don't want to believe him. But Eli and I didn't talk about the future at all. For all I know this is just a snowed in holiday fling for him. What I do know is that he's been long hailed as a commitment phobic playboy. It's one of the main reasons I fought the attraction between us so hard.

But everything that happened yesterday and this morning. It was so real. There's no way Eli would do this.

The sting of hot tears burns my eyes, but I refuse to break

down in front of Simon. That's what he wants. I know it. He's enjoying the hell out of this.

And then, the final nail in the coffin.

"You're fired Jade. I'd say take your time getting home, but Mr. Fox requested that I stay here until you're gone." With that he turns away and goes to sit on the couch, pulling out his phone and making a call.

All of my hopes and dreams lay at my feet. The perfect winter wonderland snow globe we were in has finally burst. I knew it would, but not like this. I thought we'd have more time together.

Yeah, he'd go back home. But I thought there was time. I don't want to believe Simon- in fact, I'm fairly positive he's lying. But not about firing me — that's clearly real and true. I'm so humiliated. I'm tempted to just stay here and wait for Eli. But Simon is settled in to do the same.

And what if he's right? That little worry inside me that Eli just wanted a casual fling and now that he got what he wanted, he's done with me. With us.

I don't know anything other than I need to get out of here.

"Earth to Jade. I said you need to go. Unless you want me to call security to have you removed."

I quickly walk to the kitchen, trying to keep from falling apart while I grab my phone. All the food I'd grabbed to make brunch is still on the counter. I wish I could say I just left it there, but it was drilled into me as a kid never to waste food, so I stuff it all back into the fridge.

Dressed in my leggings and then after retrieving my bag and purse, along with my coat, I call a rideshare to get the hell out of here. Unable to stand being in this house a second longer, or anywhere near Simon, I go outside to wait for the car.

It's funny that the roads were plowed today. If they hadn't, I'd still be living inside this beautiful holiday fantasy with Eli.

The perfect New Year's, the best one I've ever had. And now it's shattered.

I can't tell if it's hard to breathe because it's so cold, or because my chest aches with this pain. Had I not learned my lesson about love? I thought I'd known love before I met Eli. But now that I know him, I realize all those before him were just crushes. This, this is love. And it hurts like a bitch.

I'm tempted to call Eli. To text him. But that part of me that fears he doesn't really want me stops me.

First things first. Figure out how to get my car. Then go home, bury myself in my bed and hide forever.

19

Eli

I FINALLY PULL MY CAR BACK INTO THE CIRCULAR DRIVE-IN front of the house. A fresh coating of powder blankets the trees and roads. Looks like we might be in for another round - possibly snowing us in, again. Perfect.

Towing the car took an hour longer than it was supposed to, with the body shop running late to come get it. Then errands in town took forever. But I wanted to make sure we had everything we needed for the next few days. Because I'm going to use this time to convince Jade that we belong together.

How do you tell a woman you've known for a few months that you love her and want to spend your lives together? And that starts with me moving to Aspen permanently.

With donuts. She told me she loves them, but I wasn't sure which flavor Jade likes, so I got 12 different ones. Overkill? Possibly. But it'll be worth it to see her eyes light up when she sinks her teeth into one.

Walking through the door I expect to see Jade up and about. Hear Christmas music playing, feel a fire warming the house. I've been thinking about that scene all day. But when I open the door, it's cold and dark. All the lights are off. No fire. No music. No Jade.

"Jade!" I unload everything that's in my arms to go search for her. Maybe she's napping. After working non-stop for months, she's got a shitload of sleep to catch up on.

The bedroom and bathroom are empty. So is the kitchen, and other rooms. The back deck.

She doesn't have her car, how the hell could she have left? Why would she have left?

Last I checked we'd had the best sex of our lives not five hours ago. I go back outside - not that I think she's there, but I don't know what to look for. Even though it's snowing again, there's some faint outlines of tire tracks, too many to just be from my car.

"Fuck."

Going back in to grab my phone to call her. No answer. So I call her again, and again. But each time it goes straight to voicemail. Either her phone is off or she's screening my calls. Which I refuse to believe.

Right as I'm about to call her a third time, my phone chimes with an incoming email. The banner says it's from Simon Lewis with the Subject Line: Termination of Ms. Williamson.

What in the ever-loving fuck?!

I quickly open and scan the message.

Dear. Mr. Fox,

Thank you for choosing the Aspen Concierge Service for your staffing needs. And we always strive to exceed the high standards of our clients. It's come to my attention that one of our employees was unfortunately not fulfilling their job description in the manner that befits our organization.

My blood is boiling because I know where this is going.

So, it's with deep regret that I must let you know that Jade Williamson's employment with the ACS has been terminated, effective immediately.

We'd love to continue serving your needs during your stay in Aspen. I'll give you a call on Monday to discuss a possible replacement.

Thank you again for your trust in us.

Best,

Simon Lewis

She ran. Of course she did. I have no idea what he told her, but it was enough to make her leave without even talking to me. Without answering my calls now.

I fire off a text to her.

Me: Jade, we need to talk baby. I don't know what Simon told you, but we need to talk.

I need to go to her, talk to her. The only other place she would be is her house. I just need to find out where that is with a quick phone call.

As I run back inside to grab my keys, my phone rings. I answer without looking, "Jade!"

"Whoa dude, you alright? We've been playing phone tag, glad I caught you," Jake replies.

"No, but I will be. You better have something good for me."

20

Jade

Guess I'm going to end New Year's Day as a heartbroken mess of a person. If I cry anymore my eyes might just seal shut. I'm still wearing my same leggings and the t-shirt I borrowed from Eli. It smells like him, and I can't bear to take them off. Because if I do, it'll be like he, we, never existed.

Did the last two days really happen? Just this morning I was dreaming of a life with Eli. And now I'm sitting on my couch with a bottle of wine and a bowl of mac n cheese. Which I can't even eat because I have no appetite.

After the driver dropped me off a few hours ago, I got my official termination email from Simon. The small part of me that refused to believe it died when I saw that come through. He wasn't trying to scare me. He actually did it. Fired me. Because Eli didn't want to work with me anymore, which means that ACS doesn't want me as their employee anymore.

After that, I turned my phone off and buried my head in pillows and blankets on the couch. I've been watching reality TV. Women living in big cities who are rich. They party together and fight. Rinse, repeat. I'd rather watch nothing at all, but I can't take the silence right now. Katie is on vacation. All I have for company is our sad Christmas tree.

Through the open curtains over my windows, I see the snow falling fast and hard. They are calling for another round of storms to roll through. Thankfully it's Friday. So, I can stay in my apartment all weekend with no one the wiser. Everyone at work thinks I'm taking time off at the moment, but come Monday, they'll get the company-wide notification that I've been canned. And then the calls and texts will start. Maybe I'll just leave my phone off.

I wander into the kitchen to put the food and wine away. I can't even bring myself to look at my leftover cookies. Damnit, now Christmas cookies are ruined for me. These are stale anyways and would probably taste terrible.

Maybe I should move? I really love living here. And I thought this is where I'd put down roots, especially with the promotion I believed was coming my way. That would've enabled me to pay down debt, and then if I ever got my shit together, publish books one day. Now I gotta figure out how to pay rent soon. I have enough saved for three months, but that'll run out quickly. The job market here is saturated. This is a desirable but expensive place to live, so the options are going to be slim. I wish I could call Katie, but there's no way I'm ruining her vacation with my dumpster fire of a life.

"Fuck it, I'll eat these anyways," I mumble and tuck the tin of cookies under my arm, pour a glass of milk, and plop back on the couch. Right as I start dunking cookie number one in, a loud knock sounds at my door.

I'd normally pretend I'm not home, but a few weeks ago my neighbor lost his cat and came banging on my door to ask if I'd seen Tallulah. I helped him look outside and they were reunited in ten minutes. I bet it's him again. And I can't stand the thought that it's happened again, so I trudge over to the door and swing it open without even looking out the peephole.

Instead of my shorter and wiry elderly neighbor, I'm greeted by the very tall and broad Eli Fox. He's so handsome it hurts to look at him. His dark hair is covered with a sheen of powdery snow. His emerald green eyes are fixed on me, something like panic and hope shining in them. His lips are pressed in a thin line, as though he's been clenching his jaw. The collar of his navy wool coat is standing up framing his jawline, which is currently covered in day old scruff that on some would look sloppy. But on him, it only adds an air of danger.

Get out of your head, Jade. This isn't a fairytale.

"Can I come in?" Eli's voice is pure gravel. He's always commanding when he speaks, but he seems a little uncertain at the moment. Which throws me off as well.

Without a word, I continue standing there. Not opening the door any further. The anger I hadn't felt yet finally makes an appearance.

"Whatever you want to say I think can be said out here. I'm busy, so?"

Eli peers around my shoulder, like he doesn't know that it's obviously a lie that I'm busy. I'd already told him all my friends are out of town. And oh yea, I was just fired. Because of him.

"Baby girl, I don't know what Simon told you —."

"Don't fucking call me that," my voice cracks. And while I thought I'd cried all the tears possible, there's more just begging to be released.

"He told me exactly what you told him to. That I'd crossed a professional boundary, and you *no longer needed my services*," I say with air quotes for effect.

"I never said that. He lied to you, Jade. Do you honestly believe I'd have you fired at all? Let alone like that?"

"I didn't want to believe —"

"Please, can I come in?"

I swing the door open wide to let him in and when it shuts, I quickly walk to the kitchen to busy myself with something, anything. If I have free hands, I might hug him or something equally stupid. Does he really mean it?

"Ok, so tell me why I should believe you."

Eli lets out a frustrated sigh and rakes his hand through his hair. "The whole way here I tried to think of how to explain it to you."

I don't say anything, just allow him to continue.

"Five years ago, I met a woman, Emily. She was in the marketing department. And while I'd always had a strict no fraternization policy at the company, and especially for myself, she got under my skin. We started dating. Two months into it, I thought I was in love with her, and she with me."

Eli looks lost in the past, the pain in his voice evident.

"Turns out she was using me, passing information to my company's biggest competitor."

"My god, Eli. I'm so sorry. I had no idea."

"No one does. When I found out, I had my lawyers take care of it. I crushed the competitor by buying out 51% of their shares. I absorbed their company, kept those who were honest and loyal, and fired those who were in on the scheme."

"What happened…to her?"

"She moved. But not before signing an NDA. That's how we kept it quiet. I swore to myself, I'd never let myself get so tangled up in a woman again. I became reclusive. Rarely dated anyone, and if I did, it was never more than once. I wouldn't allow myself to get attached. Until…" Eli looks at me expectantly.

"Until?"

"Till you tripped through that door. And instead of being embarrassed, you laughed at yourself."

"Oh, I was embarrassed."

"But your laugh. Something about it - I think I fell in love with you right then."

Wait, what?

"Are you saying that you…that you *love me*, love me?!"

Eli strides, lifting me to sit on the counter, then wedges his hips between my thighs, pressing us close - chest to chest. He cups both sides of my face with his hands.

He lightly kisses my forehead. "Yes, Jade." Then the tip of my nose, "I'm saying that I love you." He hovers over my mouth, waiting for me to reply.

I can't stop myself from crying, this time happy tears. God I must look like a wreck right now, and I duck my face to wipe my cheeks and nose.

"No hiding," he says, lifting my chin up so I meet his eyes.

"Please tell me that I'm not alone in this?" he asks, searching my face for an answer.

"You're not. I always thought I knew what love was. And then I met you and realized I'd had no clue before. I know it's fast. This is crazy and doesn't make sense. But I love you too. But I don't understand how this will work. I live here, you live in California."

A huge grin lights up his face.

"I'm staying here."

"But the foundation?"

"Can be run from anywhere, Jade. And I want you to join the team."

"What? I don't know, that's all kinds of nepotism..." Surely, he's joking?

"We can put all kinds of policies in place. You won't have to report to me, so that we're not violating the rules. But only if you want. If you want to write full time, then do that. I want you to do whatever it is that makes you happy. I'll support any decision you make. As long as it's not going back to the ACS."

His mention of the ACS makes me pause. "Wait, why would I go back to the ACS? Simon fired me."

Eli gives me a knowing look, "I don't know, Simon may not be there much longer."

"Ok, we'll get back to that later, because I know you did

something. But — so you're going to move here full-time? Run the foundation from here, and you want us to be together?"

"That's the long and the short of it, baby. I'll be wherever you are. If that's Ok with you?" he says earnestly.

I'm full-on sobbing now. And reaching forward to kiss Eli. What starts off gentle quickly turns to a frenzy. You'd never know we'd only been apart 12 hours.

I pull away, catching my breath. Before we get carried away, I need to know, "Now tell me about Simon."

"That's a story for tomorrow. Just know that problem has been taken care of."

He has a devious look on his face, and something tells me I'm going to like whatever he tells me.

I wrap my legs around his waist and drape my arms around his neck. "Hey, wanna get snowed in here together?"

"Like you wouldn't fucking believe," Eli says as he lifts me off the counter and carries me towards my bedroom.

Epilogue
JADE

Three Months Later

THERE'S STILL snow on the ground, but at least the frigid tundra we've been in for months is beginning to lift. Eli wanted me to move into the house with him immediately. But I told him I needed time to spend with Katie since she's moving soon. So, I finished out my lease and moved into the house up the mountain with Eli last week.

I'm in the kitchen working on a new cookie recipe when Eli comes in from his office. He looks relaxed and happy. He's shared just how stressed he was when he was running Fox Enterprises.

Luckily, the sale of the company went off without a hitch. His board duties are minimal, and he can devote his time to the foundation. Since it launched in January, it's already funded scholarships for twenty students to pursue STEM education. I know he's got big plans for more.

I helped until it got off the ground but decided not to work for him. As much as I did enjoy it, I want to keep those parts of my life separate. Besides, I've been writing.

"How are these ones turning out?" Eli asks as he leans in to kiss me. I put a cookie up to his lips encouraging him to take a bite.

"Jesus these are good," he moans, chewing on it. "How's the book coming along?"

Now that I'm writing full time, I've had more story ideas than I can keep track of. "Good. The first draft should be done in a few months."

At first, I fought the idea of not working for a consistent paycheck. I've had a job since I was 14 and am extremely independent. But it turns out I had a case against the ACS and Simon for my wrongful termination. So rather than going to court, they settled with me.

Aspen's a remarkably small town in that everyone knows everyone. When news got out about Simon's multiple affairs, he was ruined and left the ACS. Last I heard, he'd moved to another ski town in Colorado and is probably pulling the same bullshit there. Good riddance to him.

He won't admit it, but I know Eli had something to do with Simon being exposed.

I used that settlement to pay off all my debt, with enough left over to give this writing thing a go. I know Eli wants to support me financially, but it's important to me that I pay for my own things as well. But I know how privileged I am to not have to work full-time right now.

"I'm so fucking proud of you Jade," Eli says as he gathers me in his arms, peppering kisses all over my face. "You happy?" He asks, looking down at me. Love clearly shining in his eyes.

For a writer, I still have a hard time putting into words just how happy he makes me.

"Yes. More than I can express," I say squeezing him in a hug.

"Me too, baby. Which is why I'm hoping you'll say

yes....to being my wife," he says as he backs away, a small black box in his hands. I have no idea where it came from.

"Seriously?"

Eli laughs, "Yea baby, seriously. I love the hell out of you and want to spend the rest of our lives together. I figured what better way to ask you than in the kitchen surrounded by cookies," he says with a wide grin.

It's so fast, but I don't care. It feels just right.

"Yes! Yes, I'll marry you, Eli."

He swoops me up in a bear hug and tugs my legs around his waist. He kisses me soundly, nibbling on my lips as he says, "You know, we're supposed to get one last big snowstorm later today. Wanna get snowed in together?"

The End

Acknowledgments

Holy shit, I wrote a book! When I decided to combine my love for all things romance and writing a few years ago, I seriously never thought I'd be here. Publishing was just a far-off dream. I didn't believe I could really do it.

I've been a loooong time reader of romance, and I wanted to be an author. I grew up writing and spinning fairy tales, and somewhere along the way adulthood life got in the way. I started writing again in 2021 and it was like I found my missing piece.

But there's no way I could've done this alone!

First, I want to thank my partner. In early 2021, I told him I wanted to write a book. And with every step along the way, he's been there to support me. He cheers me on when I have good writing days and crank out the words. And on days when I can't find the words, he encourages me to keep going. I couldn't have done this without you, Matt. Always and forever, more than the moon and the stars.

To my editor Brittni Van of Overbooked Author Services. Thank you for being so wonderful to work with, and for being so patient with me and my questions. You truly helped this story shine!

To Bea at Cover Apothecary, thank you for he amazing cover! The minute we spoke about this story, I feel like it just clicked, and you got my vision for it and brought it to life. You're so freaking talented, and I'm honored to call you my friend!

They say writing is a very solitary act, and that's true! But I'm so fucking lucky to have found a group of writers who started out as a sprint group, but quickly became some of my best friends. Cat Wynn, SJ Tilly, Elaine Reed and S.L. Astor, THANK YOU for all the brainstorming, late night writing sessions, listening to me complain that *I'll never make it*, and everything in between. This book, and those to come, could not have been done without you.

To my family and friends, outside the book world, I appreciate all the *how's the writing going* check-ins. They simultaneously made me want to throw up, and showed me how much you care and are interested in the things I'm interested in. I love you all. You know who you are.

And lastly, thank you to Bookstagram. I joined in early 2021, thinking I'd meet a few other new authors and figure out how to publish a book. I was so naïve going into this. It's been hard. I've doubted myself more than I believed in myself. But the community, friendship and support I've found through Bookstagram has been transformative.

Thank you, thank you, thank you. From the bottom of my heart. This is only the beginning, and I can't wait to see where my author journey takes me.

About the Author

G. Marie lives in Atlanta, GA, with her partner and the most spoiled cat in the world. Her hobbies include writing and reading romance, binge-watching baking shows and eating a ridiculous amount of cheese.

Books By This Author

Snowed in Fling

It's New Year's.

This is supposed to be my day, well week, off – a time to rest, relax and remember my company's strict no fraternization with clients policy. Because, as each day goes by, my crush Eli Fox, our most valuable client, becomes stronger and harder to ignore.

But I'm up for a coveted promotion and that means my day off has turned into a day with Eli- working. It was all good until a snowstorm left us stranded together, and in a moment of weakness, I finally gave in to the urge to kiss him.

And he kissed me back.

But I got nervous and ran…right into a snowbank.

Stuck and humiliated, there's only one person to call. And like a knight- in a- shining- SUV, Eli comes to the rescue and I spend New Year's at his luxury mountain house. And as the clock ticks closer to midnight, the fireworks between us start to ignite. I'm not sure how this is going to turn out, but I do know, this new year is going to start with a bang!

Printed in Great Britain
by Amazon